FROSTY ROBERTS
and the
GOLDEN JADE MYSTERY

By

BERNARD PALMER

MOODY PRESS

CHICAGO

ISBN: 0-8024-2883-5

Printed in the United States of America

Contents

1

The Khoo Family

THE BLAZING TROPICAL SUN cut a golden swath across the placid Malacca Straits from its resting place on the rim of the horizon. It clung to the distant sea for a moment. Already the shadows were stretching out one to the other to hide the depths of narrow streets and alleys. In a short time the sun would be no more, plunging the noisy city into darkness.

Khoo Chong knew that night was not far away, that it would reach his two American companions and him before they had covered half the distance to his home. Indeed, he had been stalling for the protective shroud of evening, and only now that its approach was imminent did he quicken his pace.

The twelve-year-old Chinese boy hurried on to the busy bridge that crossed the Singapore River, with Frosty Roberts and his cousin, Todd Burris, a few steps behind. The traffic on the wide stream below them had practically ceased, save for the *tongkangs*, nosing wearily up river to their places of

7

mooring. The clumsy boats had been shuttling back and forth all day, loading freight from the ships standing offshore and then disgorging their cargoes on the wharves, emptied one back load at a time by longshoremen. Now darkness was upon them, and they were through until the morning sun called them back to their task.

A pedicab crowded past the three boys in its haste to cross the bridge, brushing lightly against Frosty's jeans. Startled, he turned quickly to see an elderly Chinese businessman and his wife riding in the buggy-like vehicle being pushed by a bicycle. A scrawny, sallow-cheeked Malay was doing the pedaling.

"Hey," Frosty exclaimed. "How about riding in one of those?"

He had only been joking, but Khoo Chong swung to him with fear in his eyes.

"My father, he say we walk! Okay?"

Frosty's gray eyes narrowed curiously. He couldn't see why it made any difference whether they walked to the Chinese boy's home or rode in a pedicab. It wasn't that big a deal.

"Sure, it's okay. I just thought—"

"Some other time we ride in a pedicab," Chong repeated. "Tonight we walk."

Frosty couldn't understand why walking was so important that particular night. Actually he couldn't understand a lot of things about Chong and this visit to his home they were making. Even Dr. Leng had been strangely secretive when he first told them about the Chinese boy and suggested the errand to his home.

8

Dr. Leng was a long-time friend of Frosty's dad and had been helping with the research on his father's new book. The doctor had rented them rooms in a medium-priced Singapore hotel on the edge of the business district and had chartered a small boat to take them up the Malaysian coast to Penang. Even though Mr. Roberts had been concerned about taking so much time to travel up the coast by boat, he had agreed when Dr. Leng had explained that it would give him a look at a part of Malaysia he could not see otherwise. He trusted the Chinese scholar completely.

And Dr. Leng trusted the Khoo family. "Khoo Siang Ho has been a friend of mine for years," he had said. "He's an honorable man."

"Khoo Chong won't be able to come directly to the hotel to meet you," Dr. Leng had continued. "Go down to the park late tomorrow afternoon, and he will find you."

"Why?" Frosty had blurted. He had tried, but he could not keep from asking the question.

The thin line of Dr. Leng's lips had narrowed sternly. "Because that is the way Chong's father and I arranged it."

The youthful Americans still were not satisfied. They both had had questions they wanted answered—a lot of them— but the Chinese scholar's dark frown stopped the words on their lips. Disturbed, Frosty had directed his attention to his dad, hoping he would take up the questioning until they had gotten the answers that satisfied them. However, Mr. Roberts had apparently known everything that was going on.

"It's all right, Frosty," he had said quietly. "I know Siang Ho, too. He's an honorable man. I'm glad we're able to do a favor for him."

"Exactly," Dr. Leng had added. "But mind you, there is to be no talking about it—not even in your room. Do you understand?"

Frosty hadn't understood that at all. He hadn't understood anything about what they were being asked to do, especially why it had to be so secretive. The conversation had ended then, but Dr. Leng had warned them once more, just before they had left the hotel, that they must keep quiet and wait in the park for Chong.

It seemed to take days for the Chinese boy to arrive.

"I don't think he's coming at all," Todd had complained.

Frosty had jabbed him in the ribs with his elbow, a sharp reminder to remember Dr. Leng's warning.

"Well, I don't. We've been out here long enough for a dozen guys to show up. Let's go back to the hotel. I'm hungry."

"You're always hungry."

Todd had rubbed his protruding stomach with a dimpled hand. "We haven't had anything to eat since noon."

"Except for those two candy bars and a bag of peanuts and half a dozen bananas you downed."

"Well," Todd had grinned. "Hardly anything."

About that time, Chong had walked over to them. Dr. Leng had described him as a slight, lean-faced lad about their own age who would be wearing a pair of tattered shorts and a green batik shirt with yellow Malayan kites all over it. They couldn't have missed him.

"Hi," he had exclaimed, approaching them boldly. "You are Americans, no?"

"You know who we—" Todd protested. But before he had

10

been able to finish, Frosty had poked him in the ribs once more. "Oof!" The breath had swooshed out of him, and he had gasped for more.

"Yes," Frosty had acknowledged. "We're Americans."

"You like to have me show you Singapore? I make fine guide, cheap."

They had talked about price for a moment or two before Frosty agreed to go with him.

"You follow me one or two hours, and you hire me all the time." The Chinese lad had drawn himself erect. "I am the best guide in Singapore."

Frosty had started off with Chong, but Todd had just stood there.

"Come on, will you?" Frosty had said, disgust in his voice. There were times when that cousin of his was impossible.

"Let's get something to eat first."

"My father's number one son knows a good place to eat," Chong had said.

Todd still had only moved a step or two. "I'm half starved now. How long will it take to find him?"

"No time at all."

"Where is he, then?"

Chong had grinned and tapped his chest with his forefinger. "Right here."

They had left the park, cutting diagonally across the grass, and pushed their way through the crowd that surged over the wide bridge. The farther they walked, the more tense their Chinese companion became. At each corner he paused and looked in both directions. Then, as though he was talking to either Frosty or Todd, he turned to look behind them.

11

Frosty wanted to ask who he was looking for, but he didn't dare.

They walked some distance from the river to reach Bugis Street, a Chinese thoroughfare the boys had not yet visited. During the day it was an ordinary street of ordinary homes, like any other middleclass street in Singapore. But at night it changed dramatically. With the setting of the sun, display tables featuring shirts and sandals and crafts appeared.

Halfway up the block, a crowd had gathered to watch a trio of acrobats performing with the easy grace of a circus act. Behind them, a slight, perspiring individual was hawking patent medicine, every phrase parroted by a young assistant. Forest Roberts and Todd stopped to see what was going on, but Khoo Chong pushed ahead, forcing his way through the crowd. They had to hurry to catch up with him.

At one place he paused, pretending to look at some blown glass animals. But, even as he did so, he kept glancing furtively at the crowd they had just come through.

Todd sidled over to him. "What's the matter?" he asked. "Afraid someone's following us?"

The Chinese boy glanced swiftly at him in warning and shifted his attention to a delicate glass swan on the table before him.

"I think maybe I get one of these for my mother for Christmas."

Before either boy had time to reply, he returned the swan to the table and moved on. Several blocks up the busy, well-lighted street he turned down a narrow alley. At the end of the block, he turned left along a dark tunnel-like street that was scarcely wide enough for two pedicabs to meet on it. The

12

houses, huddled together on either side, were gloomy and forbidding. Frosty had the uneasy feeling that hostile eyes were peering out at them, noting their every move.

Khoo Chong's every action heightened his concern. He hurried even faster than before, keeping close to the houses on the right side of the street. Whenever anyone met them, which was seldom, he pressed against the nearest building or ducked into a doorway to stand motionless until the way was clear once more.

The American boys followed him with growing uneasiness. His secrecy and his concern that they might be followed only increased their fears. There had to be some reason for Chong's stealth.

Frosty didn't know how many corners they turned nor how long it took them to reach the Khoo family home. He didn't know where they were or what the house looked like. All he was sure about was that they were still somewhere in the residential section of Singapore and not too far from Bugis Street.

A young black-haired girl opened the door in response to Chong's quick, sturdy knock.

"It's you, Chong!" she exclaimed. "I'm so glad you're here!"

He kicked off his shoes on the mat just outside the door and stepped inside. "Where is our father?"

"He is waiting for you," she replied.

Chong moved farther into the living room. Todd would have followed him, but Frosty grasped his arm and pointed to his shoes.

"I keep forgetting."

13

The boys had kicked their shoes off when a pleasant voice sounded behind them. "There is no need for you to do that."

They turned to see a slender, smiling man manipulate his wheelchair into the long room from another part of the house.

"I'm Khoo Siang Ho," he said, introducing himself. "And these are my daughters and my wife."

Not until the introductions were complete did he turn to his son. "We were beginning to get concerned, Chong."

"We came the long way."

Fear flecked Siang Ho's dark eyes. "Then you were followed?"

"Only at first. From the bridge to Bugis Street. We lost them in the crowd."

"You are sure?"

Chong smiled, "I'm positive."

"Of course they weren't followed, Father," his older sister, Khoo Guat said. "We've all been praying that they wouldn't be."

"I know. I know. But I am glad they are safely here, anyway."

Frosty's gaze met Todd's, apprehensively.

"We are glad you boys came here with Chong," Siang Ho continued. "God has sent you here to help us."

2

Help Needed

KHOO SIANG HO was about to continue when his oldest daughter said something to him in Chinese.

"A thousand pardons," he said to the boys. "I have been so concerned about our own problems I have not even asked you to sit down. Will you forgive me for being such a poor host?"

He would say no more about the purpose of their strange visit to his home until they were comfortably seated in the living room and had been served something to drink and a plate of cake.

Todd beamed when he saw the food. "You may not know it," he told Khoo Guat, "but you've just saved my life."

"Food!" Frosty exclaimed. "That's all you ever think about."

Todd took two pieces of cake. "You know that's not true," he protested. "I think of lots of things besides eating."

"Like what?"

17

He grinned crookedly. "If I think of something, I'll let you know."

At last Siang Ho spoke. "You must greet your father for me, Forest," he said. "I met him the last time he was in Singapore."

Frosty nodded. "He said he knew you."

"And your charming mother. I understood Dr. Leng to say that she was planning to make this trip with your father."

Frosty squinted curiously at him. He hadn't realized that Chong's father knew so much about his parents. "Her sister was sick," he explained, "and she had to stay and take care of her. So Todd and I got to come."

Siang Ho smiled. "Dr. Leng is a close friend. I used to work with him before—" Instead of continuing to speak he touched his withered legs significantly. "It was while I worked with Dr. Leng that I met your father."

"I see."

The man in the wheelchair was silent for so long, the boys began to squirm uncomfortably.

"Now I must tell you why I had Chong bring you here."

He paused and the boys leaned forward expectantly.

"My father, Chong's grandfather, died last week in George Town. That's on the Island of Penang off the coast of northern Malaysia," he explained.

Frosty nodded. He knew where Penang was. They were scheduled to go there any day in the boat his dad had rented. But he didn't know how he could be very concerned about the death of Chong's grandfather. He wasn't acquainted with the elderly Chinese man who had died. In fact, two hours before, he hadn't even met Chong.

18

The older man read the perplexity in his eyes. "I have to tell you these things," he explained, "in order to make you understand why we seek your help."

"I see," Frosty replied. But he really didn't understand at all. Nothing about the Khoo family and the mysterious trip with Chong that night made sense to him.

Khoo Siang Ho seemed to sense the boys' bewilderment, but he hesitated, as though weighing the difficulties confiding in them might create. "You will remain silent about what we tell you now?" he asked.

"Sure," Todd said. "We won't say a word to anybody."

"Not even if you are pressed to speak?"

"You can depend on us," Frosty assured him. "We both know how to keep a secret."

"I am sure you do, or we would not have called on you, but we have to be so very careful. The last few days they watch everything we do."

The Roberts boy shivered.

"My father's death was a great sadness to me. I am the oldest son and wanted to attend his funeral, but they wouldn't let me."

Todd Burris thought he was referring to the doctor who had forbidden him to go to Penang because of his health. "Why?" he asked, curiously. "Because of—of the wheelchair?"

Chong's father shook his head. "No, the doctor did not care. It is because my family and I are Christians. We decided long ago to walk with Jesus Christ. My sisters are Buddhist like my father." He breathed deeply. "They know I no longer believe in worshiping our ancestors and that I wouldn't carry out the rites that are the responsibility of the oldest son. So I have been denied the place of honor as the new leader of our family. I was not even allowed to go to the funeral."

He paused momentarily. "I must tell you something about my father so you will understand why it was even harder for him to accept the fact that I am a Christian than it would be for most Buddhist fathers.

"He was not only a Buddhist, he had dedicated his working life to temple carving."

"What's that?" Frosty asked.

"When you visit the temples, you will see," Siang Ho explained. "He was a sculptor in wood who devoted his entire life to carving gates and cornices and dragons and statues of the gods for Buddhist temples. He was chosen among all the carvers of Malaysia to carve the dragons in front of the Temple of the Reclining Buddha in Penang. They were his crowning achievement. So you can see why he was so disturbed when I became a believer in Jesus Christ."

Frosty had read enough about Buddhism to know that ancestor worship was all-important. Only by being worshiped could the Buddhist be sure things were going to be easy for him in the next world. The oldest son in the family was charged with the burden of keeping the ancestor worship going. Every Buddhist home was supposed to have its god shelf and ancestor shrine, but the oldest son was the one who was to make arrangements for the special ceremonial days. He contacted the priests and bought the paper houses and cars and servants and money that were to be burned so the one who died would have those things to use in the next world.

"My father knew he was going to die soon," Siang Ho continued, "and at first he was bitter toward me and my family because our love for Jesus Christ would not allow me to worship him. He ordered me from the house when I told him I had become a Christian. I did not see him again, even when he was ill."

This was something else Frosty could not understand. Both he and Todd went to Sunday school most of the time when they were back home, but they weren't fanatical about it. He didn't see why either Siang Ho or his father would make such a big deal about it.

He had never been around anyone who talked about praying and trusting Jesus Christ the way the Khoo family did. It made him uncomfortable just listening to them.

"The day before my father died," Chong's dad went on, "he had a trusted servant write a letter to me for him. He sent it down to Singapore with a friend."

His son moved closer as though he didn't know much about the letter. "What did grandfather write you?" he asked.

"I've already told you, Chong," his father reminded him gently. "I've told you most of it, anyway. He said he knew I was a Christian and would not carry on the ancestor worship of our people. He said it bothered him that he did not have any other sons to worship him. But he realized now how much Jesus Christ must mean to me—to us all—because we were willing to put Him ahead of our family. It made him wonder if Jesus didn't represent the right way. He wished he had time enough to have me come up to Penang to explain to him about our faith and how one became a Christian."

"Do you think he was a believer before he died?" Khoo Guat broke in.

"Only God can answer that," Siang Ho said sorrowfully. "Maybe someone came to the house to show him the way."

He paused once more, thoughtfully.

"I had written to him, explaining about Jesus and becoming a Christian. I wrote twice every month even though I never heard from him. And I sent him a Bible for Christmas two years ago. I don't know if he read my letters or kept the Bible."

"Did he say anything else, Father?" Chong asked.

"He said that I was still his son and he wanted me to have my rightful heritage." He lowered his voice to a whisper. "My father's great-grandfather was a wealthy merchant who had many treasures. His most valuable was a small figurine carved from the ivory taken from the helmeted hornbill, a rare bird found in the jungles of Borneo. This figurine, of *yellow jade* as some people call the material on the bird's head, is what he has left to me."

Frosty and Todd were disappointed. They couldn't see how anything like that could be worth all the fuss.

"You mean that's what all of this is about?" the Roberts boy asked.

"It's a statuette of an elderly Chinese sage, and it's worth a lot of money," Siang Ho said. "Twenty thousand American dollars. Enough to build a new church to replace the one that burned down a few months ago."

Frosty whistled his amazement. He could see by looking around the house that they could use the money for other things—things they really needed for themselves.

"You could sure buy a lot with that much money."

"Yeah," Todd added. "Think how many chocolate malts it would get."

"There you go," Frosty chided, "putting your stomach first again. Don't you *ever* think about anything but eating?"

Siang Ho turned to his daughter. "Why don't you cut our young friend some more cake?"

"He doesn't want any," the Roberts boy said.

Todd was disappointed and showed it. "I suppose I shouldn't eat any more," he said, wistfully, "but that was mighty good. Maybe I could have just a little piece."

While Khoo Guat was bringing the cake, Siang Ho went on. "The people in our church are very poor. There is no money to build a new building if we don't use what we get from selling the figurine. We all have been praying much about it; therefore when we got the letter saying I should come up to Penang and get the little carving, we knew it was an answer to our prayers."

"Are you going to?" Frosty asked.

"In this wheelchair I would never be able to get it and get back here safely with it. It would be stolen from me before I was able to leave the island." He went on to tell them that news of the valuable artifact had already reached the kind of men who would do anything to get their hands on it. "I'm sure they are the ones who have been following members of our family for the last two or three days."

Frosty and Todd eyed each other questioningly, fear running up and down their spines. "And—and you want *us* to help you?" Frosty echoed incredulously. "Is that it?"

"Only in a small way. An important but very small way."

"Like what?"

23

"We want you to talk to your father," the man in the wheelchair explained in guarded tones. "Tell him we desperately need his help— You'll do that for us, won't you?"

He did not answer immediately.

"You'll have to be careful not to let anyone overhear you," Siang Ho added. "If word got out that your father might help us, it could ruin everything."

"You don't have to worry about that," Chong broke in. "Frosty is his father's number one son. He's smart, and you can trust him."

The corners of Siang Ho's mouth twitched. "Sometimes the number one son is like mine. A number one pain in the neck."

Chong's cheeks darkened. "Aw," he muttered. "You didn't have to say that."

The older man acted as though he hadn't even heard him. "I sent Chong to the hotel to talk to your father the other day, but when he saw that he was being followed, he wisely turned around and came back. So we got a neighbor boy to take a note to the hotel to Dr. Leng, asking that he make arrangements for you two to meet Chong in the park tonight and come here with him. Dr. Leng has advised your father that you will bring word of my request."

Frosty's eyes narrowed. He didn't know whether he appreciated that or not. "Man, if anyone saw us come here, we could get clobbered."

"Nobody knows you're here," Chong said scornfully. "I saw to that."

The young Americans didn't agree with him, but Khoo Siang Ho said they were in no danger. "Chong often guides

24

Americans around Singapore for tips. If anyone saw you leave the park with him, he wouldn't have tagged along very far before he would have been positive Chong was just showing you the sights. And it must have been successful. They didn't follow you here."

"What is it you want us to do?" Frosty asked uneasily.

"Tell your father what I have told you. Tell him everything. Ask him to consult with Dr. Leng. Then if he will agree to help, I want you to let me know."

Todd thought about that.

"I can't say I'm too excited about going through this tomorrow," he muttered.

"I have another way, one where you won't have to come out here. You can let us know," Siang Ho said. "I want you to do exactly as I tell you," he cautioned, repeating his instructions once more. "Do you understand?"

"I think so." They repeated what they had been told.

"Good. If you do exactly as I say, we will know that your father will help us."

"And if we don't?"

"We will know that he has refused."

"But he won't do that," Guat broke in quickly. "We have been praying that he would help us."

Siang Ho prayed for the two boys once more before they left, thanking God for bringing them safely to his home and asking that He would guide them safely back to their hotel. When he finished praying, he told Chong it was time for them to leave.

They were at the front door when Chong's mother appeared. She had been standing behind the heavy drapes watching the dark street. "You had better go out the other door," she said. "Those men are watching out front again!"

Her son's dark cheeks paled. "Are you sure?"

"I've been watching them for the last ten minutes."

3

On Their Own

KHOO CHONG remained motionless at the doorway for an instant.

"What should we do, Father?" he asked.

Siang Ho did not answer immediately. He pushed his thin fingers through his hair and turned in his chair to face his number one son.

"We will have to find out if they are watching both doors." He turned to his daughter. "Guat, go out the back door and go down to the stall on the corner to buy some durian. The boys will wait here until you get back."

"If she buys something to eat, Mr. Khoo," Frosty said, "those guys will know for sure that Todd's here. If he isn't eating, he's getting something to eat."

"You didn't have to say that," Todd retorted sheepishly.

Guat got some change from her father and scooted out the back door.

The American boys eyed each other with growing uneasiness. At first they had thought Chong was exaggerating his concern to give them a scare. They had even had some difficulty in believing there was such a need for secrecy as Siang Ho insisted there was. Now, however, they realized there was reason for all Chong's father was doing.

After a few minutes Khoo Guat came hurrying in, her arms loaded with the heavy, spiked fruit her father had sent her to get. She laid it on the table and rubbed her aching arms.

"I had to go to another stall up the street," she said. "And they *are heavy.*"

"Did you see those guys who are watching the house?" Frosty asked.

She shook her head. "They aren't watching the back door. I can tell you that much. I don't think they even know we have another way out of our home."

"You are *sure* you weren't followed?" her father persisted.

"I'm positive."

"That is good." His thin face reflected his relief. "Go now," he said, laying his hand on Frosty's arm. "And God be with you!"

The youthful Americans slipped out the back door with Chong.

"Man, it's dark out here!" Todd exclaimed.

"S-sh!" Their Chinese friend put a finger to Todd's lips, warning him to silence.

They moved stealthily along the narrow walk that led to the gate in the towering cement fence that enclosed the back yard. Chong opened it, wincing at the protesting shriek of metal against metal.

He then guided them along the narrow alley at a brisk pace.

30

Frosty was sure the men who were watching the front would have heard the gate open and dashed after them. Every now and then he glanced over his shoulder, trying to see if they were being followed. He had no indication they were being trailed.

Their Chinese friend took them back to downtown Singapore by another way, hurrying them through the darkened and all but empty streets. It wasn't long until they were within a block of their hotel.

"I don't think I'd better go any nearer," he said.

Todd's eyes widened. "You mean you're afraid to go over there because you think somebody may be waiting for us at the hotel?" he demanded. "What about us? Is that any way to treat your friends?"

"I just don't want them to see us together, that's all." He was whispering now, tensely. "My father said I should stay away from the hotel so if I am followed, the guys won't get the idea there's any connection between our family and your father. That's in case he decides to help us."

In spite of Chong's insistence that they had not been followed the boys covered the distance to the hotel fearfully. Not until they were safely in their room did they relax.

"Man, oh man!" the fat one puffed heavily. "I'm glad we're back here safely."

"You and me both." Frosty leaned against the desk. "I wouldn't have been surprised if we'd been grabbed before we got to the hotel and were carried off."

"Now you're real comforting," Todd said. "We're not finished with this business yet, you know."

"It'll be dad's baby after tomorrow night."

"We hope——" Todd added.

The next evening the boys left the hotel shortly after seven o'clock, carrying a sky rocket and a package of fire crackers. They had told George Roberts the purpose of their visit to the Khoo home and asked if he would help them. At first he wasn't sure he wanted to get involved. Later, after discussing the matter with Dr. Leng, he agreed.

"But only on the condition that it doesn't interfere with our research. We've got a lot of work to do if we are to finish in another two months."

As they crossed the busy street outside their hotel Frosty glanced at his watch. They had to hurry if they were going to make their way through the crowd to the park in time to send up the signal at 8:15.

They walked half a mile or more, crossing one street and then another before reaching the park at the mouth of the river. Once there they moved quickly along the winding path to the bank. It was well lighted, and there were people everywhere.

"I don't like this idea much," Frosty murmured.

"Neither do I. I'd rather go get something to eat."

"You would!"

Exactly at 8:15 they set off the sky rocket. It zoomed out over the water to a height of forty or fifty feet before exploding in a shower of light.

"Here," the Roberts boy said, "help me with these fire crackers."

An elderly woman on a park bench not far away was indignant about the noise. "I don't know what the police are about that they will allow such carrying on," she said loudly to her companion. "If I could find an officer, I'd make a complaint."

Todd didn't like the sound of that. He grasped his companion by the arm. "Come on, let's get out of here!"

"What's the hurry?"

"Take a look at that woman over there. She's about to explode like those fire crackers. And I know who's going to get blown up if she does!"

"Just a minute," he said reluctantly. He was still looking around, trying to see whether Khoo Chong or his sister were somewhere in the park. But there was no sign of them. The only other person in the vicinity who looked as though he was interested in what was happening was a gaunt, spindly individual with hawk-sharp features, who was standing near one of the park's statues. When he saw that Frosty was staring at him, he started forward hurriedly, his long, scissor-like stride cutting the distance between himself and the boys.

"Come on!" Frosty gasped. "Let's get out of here!"

With that he whirled and dashed into the crowd. His cousin Todd wasn't built for running. Before they reached the edge of the park, the fat one was laboring like a steam engine.

"Frosty!" he panted. "Take it easy, will you!"

"That guy's still after us!"

"I—I don't know why I let myself get mixed up in this mess in the first place!" Todd muttered as they dashed between two cars and leaped to the safety of the curb on the other side of the street.

"I know. You'd rather eat!"

"Now that you mention it, I would. A lot rather!"

33

"Well, don't stop to eat now, or you won't have to worry about it any more! That guy looked dangerous!"

"A lot of comfort you are."

They were two blocks from the park when Frosty finally slowed and glanced over his shoulder. "I don't think he's following us any more."

"Let's not stop to find out."

They turned another corner before they finally quit running. Neither Todd nor Frosty thought the tall stranger was still after them, but they didn't feel entirely easy about it until they were in their room on the seventh floor.

George Roberts was waiting impatiently for them.

"I'm glad you guys got back when you did," he said. "I was afraid I was going to have to leave a note for you."

"You're going somewhere?"

He nodded. "We just had a phone call from Djakarta, Indonesia. One of the men we've been wanting to interview has finally agreed to talk to us, providing we begin tomorrow. So we've got to leave tonight."

"But what about Penang?" Todd asked.

"I talked it over with Dr. Leng. He thinks it would be better for you boys to go up to the island on the boat. As soon as we finish in Djakarta, we'll fly up to George Town to meet you."

"What about the promise we made to Khoo Chong's father?" Frosty wanted to know.

"I'm sorry about that," his dad replied, "But I only agreed to help him if it would not interfere with my research." He paused momentarily. "Maybe we can help them when we get back."

34

At that moment Dr. Leng came in. He had just talked with Captain Tham Hin Kheong, the owner of the little boat they had chartered to take them up the coast to Penang.

"He has agreed to take the boys up to the island and let them stay on the boat until we get there."

"But what about Khoo Chong and his family?" Frosty asked. "We just signaled to them that we would help them."

The wrinkles about the slender Chinese scholar's face deepened with concern. "I have taken care of that, too."

The boys wanted to ask him how he had gotten word to the Khoo family, but he and Frosty's dad were so busy there was no time for that.

"Now, do you remember the name of the boat?" George Roberts said as they were ready to leave.

"It's the *Bird of Paradise*."

"Here," Dr. Leng said, "I've written the name of the boat and the place it's docked, together with the Captain's name. They're in both English and Chinese. If you happen to get a pedicab driver who doesn't speak English, you can give him this."

Frosty put the note in his wallet. "And we're to be there at seven o'clock sharp?"

The next morning the boys dragged themselves sleepily out of bed at 5:30 and went down to breakfast. Half an hour or so later they were in front of the hotel waiting for a pedicab. The dew of the night was beginning to flee, chased away by the tropical sun.

"I sure hope that character who was after us last night has given up by now," Todd said, trying to satisfy himself that

35

the man who had been after them the night before was no-where in sight.

Frosty did not answer his cousin. Instead he started towards a pedicab that was moving their direction. As far as he was concerned, the sooner they got out of Singapore the better.

"You speak English?" he asked the pedicab boy.

"You betcha my life."

Frosty bargained briefly with him before agreeing on a price, and he and Todd got in. The city was just beginning to come to life as the driver pedaled up the street. A few cars were beginning to move across town, and the streets were already dotted with people on their way to work. Most of the eating stalls they passed were crowded with people having breakfast before going to their jobs.

The boys had not seen the *Bird of Paradise* before, but as they neared the docks, they were able to pick her out. She was an old, snub-nosed boat looking much like the tugs that worked the harbors of Hoboken and San Francisco: a squat, low-riding craft that had little speed but evoked a sturdy confidence that she would get where she was going.

"Here we are," the pedicab driver said, grinning. *"The Bird of Paradise.* And I get you here on time, I betcha."

They paid him and approached the boat.

The captain was not in sight. Only a bony old man, bare to the waist, was visible. He was sitting cross-legged on the deck, working with a coil of heavy line. They both spoke to him, but he scowled wordlessly.

"Man, he's not very friendly," Todd murmured as they pushed past him.

"I don't think he understands us."

36

The younger boy shivered. "Let me clue you. I don't understand him, either."

The captain had come out of the pilot house and greeted them.

"I see you're right on time." His smile was friendly but humorless.

"Dr. Leng said we should be here at seven o'clock."

"We are to leave at seven," Captain Tham repeated, "if that new cabin boy shows." He went to the railing and looked up the street. "My regular cabin boy came to me last night and asked if a friend could make the trip in his place. If I'd known he would disappoint us, I'd never have agreed to it." He glanced at his watch once more. "We'll wait another ten minutes for him. If he doesn't show up, we'll leave. I'll do the cooking myself."

The minutes passed slowly.

"Here's your chance, Todd," Frosty said. "You can volunteer to cook and spend *all* your time in the kitchen on this trip."

"You've got me all wrong," his cousin retorted. "I like eating, not cooking."

A short time later, the captain approached the boys. "Well, it looks as though he's not coming. We'll shove off."

He turned and spoke to the old man, "We're ready to go now, Yeo Seng Chi."

The old fellow disentangled his legs and got up, hobbling over to loosen the lines that secured the little boat to the dock. At that moment Frosty spotted a slight young figure darting past a pedicab and pushing through the crowd in their direction.

37

"There's Khoo Chong!" he exclaimed.

The Chinese boy jumped aboard, panting heavily.

"Who are you?" Captain Tham demanded harshly. "And what are you doing here?"

"I'm the new cabin boy!"

4

The "Bird of Paradise"

ANGER DISTORTED Captain Tham's weathered features. He glared at Khoo Chong. "You're late!" he rasped. "I sent you word that our sailing time was seven o'clock sharp this morning. You knew that, didn't you?"

Chong was apologetic. "I had a long way to come. I'm sorry if I delayed you."

"Another two minutes, and we'd have left without a cook!" He acted as though he was about to tell Chong he didn't need him. Then he softened a little. "It is good you showed when you did," he said, "or you'd have been out of a job."

An instant later the engines started, and Chong leaped to finish loosening the line that secured the bow to the dock. The wizened old Chinese, who was at the stern, pulled himself erect.

"Avast there!" Yeo Seng Chi roared in English. "Stop! I handle the lines!"

Frosty and Todd stared at him. They hadn't suspected he could speak anything other than Chinese. Chong stepped

41

back and waited for the old man to hobble forward to free the *Bird of Paradise* from her mooring. Once that was accomplished, he scrambled aboard with surprising agility, and the boat backed away from the dock. Skillfully the captain eased her forward, threading her among the heavily loaded *tongkangs* that were moving towards the wharves, where the stevedores were waiting to unload them.

Frosty found himself on the deck beside the crusty, unfriendly sailor.

"I didn't know you spoke English," he said.

Chi glared at him and loosed a torrent of Chinese before turning on his heel and stalking to the stern where he stood alone.

The Roberts boy eyed him curiously. "What was that all about?" he asked Khoo Chong.

"He was swearing at you for being so nosy. He said it's none of your business whether he speaks English or not."

Frosty couldn't figure out why the old Chinese sailor disliked him so much, but he and Todd were much more concerned about Chong and how he happened to be working on the *Bird of Paradise.*

"You didn't say anything about sailing with us when we saw you the other night," he said. "What are you doing here?"

His eyes warned Frosty to silence.

Todd looked as though he was about to take up the questioning, but Khoo Chong sidled toward the pilot house.

"I think the captain wants me," he said. "I'll come back and talk to you later."

When the boys were alone, they moved to the rail and

42

looked out over the harbor at the freighters from a dozen nations rocking silently at anchor.

"What's the deal with Khoo Chong?" Todd asked. "He acts as though he hardly knows us."

"Why should he be that way out here?" Todd wondered. "There's nobody on board to hear us."

"There's the captain and *him*." He jerked his head in the direction of the deck hand.

Todd couldn't believe his cousin was serious. "An old guy like that couldn't cause us any trouble."

"Maybe," Frosty acknowledged, "and maybe not. But we can't take any chances. Besides, we promised that we wouldn't let *anyone* know. We've got to keep our word."

The fat one shook his head. "I don't get this business."

They were still talking in hushed tones when Chong approached them. "Hi, there! Anybody ready to eat a little something, maybe? Anybody want any orange juice or peanut butter sandwiches or chocolate milk?"

"He is." Frosty gestured towards Todd. "He's always ready to eat."

"What've you got that's good?"

"It is all good!" Chong countered loudly. "My father's number one son is number one cook. You come down to the galley. You'll see."

As they left the deck he spoke to the old sailor in Chinese. Frosty could not understand him, but he knew he had asked the deck hand to join them. The elderly, frozen-faced Yeo Seng Chi glared at them and continued working.

Once in the galley where their voices were muffled by the

43

dull throb of the engines, he poured some chocolate milk for the boys, and the three of them sat down together.

"I didn't want to act as though I didn't know you guys when we were up on deck just now," he said, leaning forward and speaking just above a whisper. "But it's like my father told you. We can't take chances."

"How come you're here with us on the boat?" Todd asked. "That's what I want to know."

"When Dr. Leng sent the cabin boy of the *Bird of Paradise* to our house last night to tell us I should take his place on the trip today, we knew something had happened. Especially when he came only an hour or so after you had signalled that your dad would help us. So it was decided that the number one son in the Khoo family would come to the rescue."

"You mean *you're* going to get the figurine and take it home with you?" Frosty asked.

"What's wrong with that?" His eyes were twinkling with excitement. "I'm intelligent and clever and handsome."

"Oh, sure," the Roberts boy scoffed.

"Now you've hurt me. I'll never be the same again." The laughter faded from his youthful features. "I'm really not joking about getting the figurine. My father decided it might be safer for me to bring it back to Singapore than it would for your dad to do so. The thieves will be less apt to suspect us."

Todd squinted at him. "What do you mean, *us?*"

"You're going to help, aren't you? Isn't that what you promised?"

"I don't know." He rolled his eyes in mock horror. "Did we, Frosty?"

"We'll have to see what Chong's got in mind."

44

"It's very simple. When we get to George Town, we will go to my grandfather's house, pick up the figurine, and go back to the boat and hide it. There's nothing hard about that."

"You hope there's nothing hard about it," Todd retorted. "There are still those guys who're trying to steal it, you know."

Chong would have replied, but Yeo Seng Chi came in just then. He scowled at Frosty before directing his attention to the cabin boy, speaking in Chinese.

"Sure," Chong answered in English. "I'll fix you some tea."

No one spoke until the deck hand went topside once more, a cup in his hand.

"That guy gives me the shivers," Frosty said.

"He's just a little crotchety, that's all," their Chinese friend said.

"I don't know about that. When he looks at me, I get the feeling he'd like to chop me up and use me for fish bait."

Todd picked up another cookie and broke it in half.

"You don't suppose he overheard what we were saying, do you?" he asked.

"What makes you ask that?" Frosty wanted to know.

"He had a funny look on his face when he came in here just now, as though he knew more than he was letting on."

"That couldn't be. No one on deck could hear what we're saying with the engines making so much noise."

"Unless he already knew about the figurine and guessed why you're working on board as cabin boy."

Chong still didn't think there was anything disturbing about the deck hand's manner. The American boys didn't agree with him but said no more about it.

45

"Just the same," Frosty said when they were alone, "we're going to keep our eyes on him. I still don't trust him."

Todd turned and leaned against the railing. "I sure can't get excited about helping get that yellow jade carving back to Singapore," he said. "I'd feel different if Khoo Siang Ho was going to use the money for his family, but he's not. He's going to build a *church* with it."

"I know."

"Did you ever hear anything so stupid? He's so crippled he can't even work very much. He must be out of his mind to want to put everything into a church."

Frosty did not reply immediately. He thought he felt the same as Todd did about the Khoo family putting all that money into a church, but it bothered him that the whole family was keen on it. That was something he couldn't understand. He knew he wouldn't like it if his dad were going to give so much money away. There were so many things he wanted he'd be furious if his dad had the money and then gave it away. He wanted a color television and a snowmobile and a boat and—

He was sure there were lots of things Chong would like to have, too. But he and Guat didn't say anything about that. They seemed as excited as their folks were about getting the money so they could have a new church.

There was something different about the Khoo family. They talked a lot about Jesus Christ and praying and things like that. They didn't seem to be the same as most of the people Frosty knew. He couldn't figure it out.

"I'm going to talk to Chong the first chance I get," he said aloud.

46

"About what?"

"A lot of things."

There was no chance for him to question their Chinese friend the rest of the afternoon. He fixed supper early and they all went down in the galley to eat, all except Chi, who took his turn at the wheel so the captain could have supper with the boys. Later, he came and sat down at the table and gulped his food, not even acknowledging that anyone else was in the galley with him.

While he ate, Frosty and Todd helped Chong with the dishes before going back up on deck. Their Chinese friend joined them. For a time they stood at the stern railing, looking out over the choppy straits. The sun was almost down, and the sea was taking on a dark, forbidding hue.

"There's something I've been wanting to ask you," Frosty said. "Does your dad really plan on giving all that money away when he sells the figurine?"

"You mean to build a church? Sure, he does. That's the reason we're so anxious to get it. We have to have a new building if we're going to keep our church going, and the people don't have enough money to pay for it."

Frosty gazed at the boy intently. "How do you feel about that? I mean, doesn't it make you mad?"

"Why should it?"

"Think of all the things you could buy. Think of everything you need."

Khoo Chong was perplexed. "We don't need anything," he said. "We have a nice house and plenty of clothes to wear and all the food we can eat."

"That's not what I mean. You don't even have a car."

47

Chong took a moment or two in answering him. "Building a church means a lot more to us than a car or anything else we could buy."

Frosty's gaze bore into his. "Why?" he demanded.

Chong's face twisted thoughtfully. "I don't know for sure if I can explain it to you or not. You'd almost have had to see how things used to be around our place for you to understand why we feel like we do. "My father never smiled. Nobody else in the house dared to laugh or joke. He was so bitter about being in a wheelchair that he punished us if we ever showed that we were having fun. Then a Christian friend started visiting us, and my father gave his heart and life to Jesus. It was—" he paused and began again. "It was just as though somebody opened the windows and let the sunshine in. My father was happy again.

"It wasn't long until my mother became a Christian. Guat was next and then me. Our hearts began to sing. My father's heart began to sing. And we were happy again.

"I could never explain to anyone how much Jesus Christ has done for us. He's not only saved us so we will go to heaven, but he's made us happy now. He's helped us to overcome our troubles. Building a church for Him means everything to our whole family!"

Frosty fell silent. What Chong said tugged at his own heart. He didn't understand everything his new friend said. When he thought about it, he realized he didn't understand much of it. But it would be great to have what Chong had.

The Chinese boy's lips parted as though to speak once more, but he straightened suddenly, staring out across the water.

48

"Somebody's coming!" he exclaimed tensely.

"What's so strange about that?" Todd asked. "We've seen boats all day."

"I know, but not like this one! And not without any running lights on!"

The dark shape in the distance was speeding straight for them from half a mile or so away.

"I'm going to tell the captain," Chong exclaimed. "He'd better start sounding the fog horn before they run us down!"

Fear leaped to Captain Tham's eyes as his Chinese cabin boy told him about the boat that was roaring towards them. "Are you sure?"

"Of course I'm sure! And he's coming right at us!"

"Pirates!" the captain shouted. He shoved the throttles forward.

1092

5

A Pirate Chase

THE STERN of the *Bird of Paradise* squatted lower in the water, and the wake deepened as the sudden burst of power thrust her forward with increased speed. The deep, throaty snarl of the engines became a roar as the sturdy boat raced for the uncertain safety of the Malaysian shore. Stunned into silence, Frosty and Todd stared with widening eyes at the dark shape that was coming their direction from the shadows of Sumatra.

The Roberts boy was sure he must have misunderstood Captain Tham. This wasn't the seventeen hundreds when bandits roamed the seas. This was the twentieth century, a day when pirates were gone.

"The captain has to be kidding!" he exclaimed, raising his shaking voice so he could be heard above the roar of the engines. "There aren't any pirates today!" Even as he spoke, he read the truth in Khoo Chong's somber face. "Are there?"

"I wish there weren't!" The Chinese lad answered, squint-

51

ing in the spreading darkness at the craft that seemed to be drawing nearer. "They hide out in the jungle across the straits in Sumatra and raid the boats that travel the straits."

Frosty wiped the sweat from his forehead. "You can't mean it."

"It's the truth. Let a fishing boat from Malaysia get out too far, and they nail her and hold the men for ransom—if they're lucky."

Todd caught the ominous inflection in his voice. "And what if they don't have any money?" he asked.

"Sometimes they're never heard of again. And sometimes they're found floating face down in the straits or along shore."

"You're sure an encouragement."

"That's only if they catch them," Chong retorted.

The captain called for him just then, bellowing over the roar that enveloped them. "You, Chong! Come here!"

Frosty and Todd followed him, crowding into the pilot house behind him. "Yes?" the Chinese boy responded.

Captain Tham's perspiring hands trembled on the wheel, and the color had fled his cheeks. "Are they getting any closer?" he demanded harshly.

"A little."

Frosty realized that was true, but hearing it stated chilled him.

With his left hand the captain reached over and flicked on the radio shouting into the mike in Chinese.

"What's he saying?" Todd wanted to know.

"He's calling for help," Chong explained, his body tense. "He says the pirates are closing in on us, and he doesn't know how long it will be until they board us. He says it's the second time he's called for help, and if they don't come soon, we'll be taken by the pirates."

Todd gulped. "Is it that bad?"

"What do you think?"

As though for answer the boat behind them fired a shot over the cabin of the *Bird of Paradise.*

"Hey!" Todd cried, "those guys *do* mean business."

"It's just a warning for us to stop!" Captain Tham exclaimed over his shoulder.

"You're going to take it, aren't you?"

"Get down!" he ordered. "All three of you!"

The boys hadn't expected their Chinese captain to continue his wild dash for freedom, but he did. Without touching the throttle, he heaved hard on the wheel, forcing the *Bird of Paradise* to swerve to starboard. A moment later he reversed himself, throwing the sturdy boat to port. The boys were slammed hard against the bulkhead as she heeled over.

The pirate boat fired at them once more, closer this time.

"Wow!" Todd exclaimed. "That was close!"

The boys looked up at Captain Tham, incredulous. Frosty had been sure he would cut their speed when the pirates fired at them, but he continued to speed toward a village harbor, taking evasive action when the other craft started firing at them.

Khoo Chong, who was lying on the deck beside Frosty, began to pray, asking God to help them escape the pirates and get safely to the Malaysian village. Frosty could only hear enough to know Chong was praying, but his Chinese friend's calmness surprised him. Chong was frightened, he was sure of that, but not half so frightened as the Roberts boy was him-

53

self. His voice was even and well controlled, and he lay quietly on the deck. Todd, on the other side of him, was twitching convulsively, and his breathing was heavy and labored.

Somehow Frosty was comforted by Chong's praying. That surprised him, too. Always before when the subject of Christ or praying or church came up, he was disturbed by it. He wondered if Todd felt the same.

They were two miles or so from shore when a voice crackled over the radio.

"Ah!" Captain Tham exclaimed aloud. "It's about time!"

"What did he say?" Todd demanded.

"A Malaysian patrol boat is on its way from the village," Chong interpreted.

The boys got cautiously to their feet and peered into the heavy shadows ahead.

"Do you see it?" Todd asked, fearfully.

"Not yet, but she's there," the captain said confidently.

"Hey!" Frosty cried. "The pirates have turned around. They're going back!"

Captain Tham laughed. "They must have a radio, too." He glanced at Chong. "You can stop praying now."

At first Frosty thought he was being sarcastic. Looking back, however, he wasn't sure. The captain sounded as though he was completely serious.

Although the pirate boat had stopped chasing them and had even disappeared in the darkness Captain Tham did not slacken speed. He kept the *Bird of Paradise* racing at full throttle until they reached the village harbor.

54

"Well," the Captain said, relief evident in his manner, "we made it."

"What are we going to do now?" Frosty asked.

"I'm going to the temple and burn some joss sticks for our good luck," he said. "Then I'm going to come back here and wait until morning."

Once at the dock, he turned to Khoo Chong. "Want to go with me?"

The Chinese boy shook his head. "I am a Christian," he explained.

The friendliness in the Captain's eyes gave way to contempt. "Oh," he said. "And who will worship your father when he dies?"

"He is a Christian, too."

"And your grandfather?"

Chong had no answer for him.

They left the little fishing village the next morning, feeling their way cautiously up the coast. Captain Tham had put out to sea several miles the day before. Now, however, he stayed much closer in, putting just enough distance between them and the shore to avoid the reefs.

The boys kept a wary watch of the western horizon, half expecting another pirate boat to come after them.

"We don't have to worry about pirates as close to shore as we're running," the captain informed them. "They won't come in here."

"Maybe not," Frosty said, "but I'll be glad when we get to Penang, anyway."

Yeo Seng Chi, who happened to be close enough to overhear him, looked his direction, sneering.

"You are very brave, you young westerners," he said.

Frosty caught the sarcasm but did not reply.

Toward afternoon of the third day they reached the island of Penang. They put in at the George Town harbor, went through customs, and made their way to one of the docks where they berthed the *Bird of Paradise.* Khoo Chong looked at his watch.

"Do you have anything for me to do the rest of the afternoon?" he asked.

The burly skipper shook his head. "Just so you're back here in time to fix supper for us."

Frosty and Todd left the boat with Chong, moving past the weary stevedores who were loading smoky bales of rubber aboard the *tongkangs.*

"What are we going to do now?" Todd asked, looking nervously around.

"We'll go to my grandfather's house," he said. "I'm anxious to get that over with."

"Me, too," Frosty added.

They walked along the busy street that was liberally sprinkled with European tourists and turned toward the residential district, passing a grimy temple. Todd and Frosty paused on the lip of the courtyard, curiously surveying the scene. The temple was set well back from the street, making room for a row of stalls on either side where joss sticks and paper money and fruit for sacrifices were sold. Two huge granite lions were scowling fiercely from their marble pedestals, and the furnace for burning the paper money was billowing smoke. The boys could see the yellow flames through the crack in the rusty side.

"Is this the kind of a place Captain Tham went to the other night?" Todd asked.

Chong nodded. "Come on. We've got to hurry, or we'll be late getting back."

Reluctantly they left the temple area and went with Chong. It had been several years since he had been to his grandfather's home, but he had no difficulty in finding it. The family had lived on Penang for several generations, and the house was fairly close in. It was less than a ten-minute walk from the temple.

"It's just around the next corner."

"What do we do when we get there?" Todd wanted to know.

"See my grandfather's servant and have him give us the figurine."

"Is that all?" Frosty asked. He was somewhat disappointed. After all the secrecy it didn't seem right that getting the valuable piece of jade could be so simple. He felt let down.

As they drew close, they were surprised to see a police vehicle parked in front of one of the houses and a crowd of people in the fenced yard.

"It looks as though there's some sort of trouble at that place," the fat one observed.

"That's my grandfather's!" Khoo Chong cried, hurrying forward. He approached the first man he met. "What's going on?"

The stranger shrugged indifferently. "Somebody broke into the place, I guess. The venerable grandfather who lived there died a week ago. Now someone has desecrated his home by breaking in."

The boys gasped. "Did they steal anything?" Frosty demanded.

The tall Chinese glared at him as though he, a westerner, had no right to ask such a question. Deliberately he turned away.

6

A Mysterious Map

FROSTY AND HIS COUSIN moved to the forbidding iron fence that enclosed the front courtyard as Khoo Chong casually pushed his way through the open gate and the curious, noisy crowd and made his way to the door of his grandfather's house. It was an old frame building, weathered by countless rainy seasons and the scorching tropical sun. There was an iron grating at the door and bars over each window, mute evidence of the thieves to be found in the area.

Although the boys could not see it, Chong had told them that a god-shelf was just inside the front door, the shrine to the departed ancestors of the Khoo family. There was a holder for joss sticks at one side, and at least while his grandfather was alive, there was always food on the little altar.

Now the front grating had been pushed aside and the door was open. Police were shouldering in and out of the house, carrying out their duties.

"You know," Todd whispered, "Chong's dad has got to be right. Somebody is after the figur—"

Frosty jabbed a sharp elbow into Todd's ribs so savagely that he grunted. "What'd you do that for?"

The Roberts boy did not answer him. The people around them were chattering in Chinese and Malay, giving no hint that they had heard or understood. Yet, there was always the possibility that they had been overheard by someone who mattered.

Chong rejoined them presently, concern indelibly branded on his young face.

"Did they steal anything?" Frosty asked.

"Nobody knows for sure." His voice was guarded and hushed. "The police are talking to my grandfather's servant now, trying to find out if anything of real value is missing."

After a few minutes the crowd lost interest and began to disperse. Two or three people at a time turned and sauntered away until only a handful remained.

"How long are we going to hang around here?" Todd asked presently.

"Just a minute," Chong said.

Todd rubbed his protruding stomach with a chubby hand. "Man, if I'd known we were going to stay so long, I'd have brought a sandwich."

"I'll be right back. Then we'll go to the boat and fix supper."

The Chinese boy edged forward as though he had no other purpose than curiosity. At the doorway he looked about, quickly. Satisfying himself that he had not attracted attention he slipped inside. Moments later he rejoined his American companions.

"It is not exciting around here," he announced. "Let's go."

Frosty and Todd knew Chong had had a reason for going into the house. They wondered about it but did not mention it, and neither did he until they were some distance away from any of the people who had been at his grandfather's.

They crossed the narrow street and walked past a row of small shops selling a variety of wares: noodles or sandals or fish or funeral supplies. A group of small boys were playing at the curb and called out to Chong. He answered them but did not slacken his brisk pace. When he and his friends were two blocks away, he glanced quickly about to be sure no one was within listening distance.

"I've got something here," he said softly.

"The figurine?" Frosty asked.

An almost indefinable shake of his head spoke for him. "But I got something else." He fished a tightly folded piece of paper from his pocket.

"What is it?"

"A note my grandfather's servant gave to me." With that he returned it to his pocket.

"Come on," Frosty exclaimed. "What gives? We're in this, too, you know."

"We can't take a chance on looking at it here where the guys who broke into grandfather's house may see us. We'll have to wait until we get back to the boat and are sure nobody's watching us."

"Do you think it's important?" Todd asked, sounding as though he hoped it wasn't.

"Of course it is," Frosty retorted. There were times when he got so disgusted with his cousin he'd like to disown him. "Why else would Chong have to be so careful with it?"

"Did he *tell* you to be careful with it?" Todd persisted.

Chong nodded. "He didn't exactly say it out loud, but he was very careful to give it to me when no one was looking. It's important, all right."

"I was afraid of that," Todd murmured.

Frosty Roberts shivered and glanced furtively over his shoulder to see if anyone was following them. Todd was doing the same. If they were being tailed, however, it was skilfully done. They saw no one who even seemed to be suspicious.

Chong acted as though there wasn't a remote possibility that they were being watched. He increased the pace without looking either direction except to cross the street when they reached a corner.

Captain Tham was waiting for Chong in the pilot house of the *Bird of Paradise* when they came aboard. He scowled accusingly at his watch.

"I told you to be back early."

"I'll fix supper right away."

Captain Tham grumbled something under his breath and turned back to the log book he was working on.

"Come on," Chong said, touching Todd on the elbow. "I've got to get to work."

Frosty Roberts had been staring at the captain, but as they turned to go to the galley, he looked up directly into the eyes of the Chinese seaman. He hadn't known the old man was anywhere around, and it startled him. The hair on the back of his neck bristled, and he broke into a sweat as Yeo Seng Chi's cold, hateful stare bore into him.

"I tell you, Chi was listening to everything that was said

64

when we talked to the captain," Frosty whispered hoarsely when he and his companions were safe in the galley of the little boat, away from prying eyes and ears.

"He didn't find out anything," Chong answered, "except that the captain is mad about something. And he probably knew that already."

"But why would he even try to hear what was going on? That's what I want to know."

Frosty was somewhat disturbed that the others didn't share his concern. They acted as though they didn't even notice how Yeo Seng Chi felt toward Todd and him.

"Where's that note your grandfather's servant gave you?" Todd whispered.

Khoo Chong was already fishing it from his pocket. As he unfolded the single sheet of paper, young Roberts went over and drew the shade.

"Nobody's going to see us from there," Chong said, laughing, "unless he comes up in a boat."

"Maybe not, but I'm not taking any chances."

The Chinese lad spread the paper on the table and the American boys crowded close, staring intently at it.

"It's not a letter!" Frosty exclaimed. "It's a map!"

"Of what?" Todd asked.

"I don't know, but it's got something to do with that figurine."

They studied it for several minutes, trying to decipher it. The paper was old and deeply creased, as though it had been hidden in some tiny resting place for many years. It was so soiled and greasy that it was difficult to make out parts of the drawing and markings. There were a few Chinese characters at the bottom, but of course, **Frosty and Todd** didn't know what they said.

"Does it give any hint as to the general location?" Frosty asked.

Chong shook his head.

"Is there *anything* to give a clue where it is."

"Only this inscription, 'The greater the man, the greater his responsibility to his ancestors.' "

"That sounds like he's telling you that you ought to worship him," Frosty observed.

Todd repeated the inscription thoughtfully. "It might mean something to you, but it sure doesn't mean anything to me."

Chong studied the map once more. He was about to give up when he saw something at the bottom along one end.

"Wait a minute," he exclaimed. "What's this?" He rubbed a smudge of dirt with his forefinger. "There's something here—some Chinese characters I didn't see before." After a minute or two he read them aloud, hesitantly. " 'Buddha gives long life to those who make their sacrifices and observe the holy days.' " He paused. "Why would grandfather write that on the note?"

"You told us yourself that he was upset that your father is a Christian and wouldn't be worshiping the way he had. Maybe he's trying to tell you that you ought to go back to it," Frosty said again.

Chong shook his head. "No, there's got to be another reason. This was written a long time ago, before my father gave his heart to Jesus Christ."

Todd was impatient. "If that isn't it, what does it mean?"

66

Khoo Chong bent over the map once more.

"I know!" he cried excitedly. "He's trying to tell us that the piece of jade is hidden at the temple where he used to worship!"

"Are you sure?"

"I'm positive." He was so excited his finger was trembling as he pointed. "Here are the stalls that sell joss sticks and fruit and oil for the sacrifices, and here's the vendor who has the paper money." He pulled in a deep breath. "And here are the two carved granite lions that stand in the courtyard in front of the temple."

The boys eyed each other questioningly.

"What *does* it mean?" Todd demanded.

"There's only one thing it could mean," Frosty retorted. "The jade carving is hidden somewhere around the temple, and Khoo Chong's grandfather left this map to tell where it is."

Khoo Chong was not even listening. He continued to pore over the tattered sheet of paper his grandfather's servant had given to him.

"Here's where it is," he whispered at last, pointing to the location of one of the carved granite lions. "Here's a tiny figure which means 'bird.'"

"Under that?" Todd asked. "If that's where it is, we're not going to have such an easy time getting our hands on it."

"There are some notations here I can't quite figure out," Chong went on. "It says 'second row, four over.' That doesn't make sense to me."

"Sounds like a seat for a football game," Todd put in.

"It doesn't add up," the Chinese boy continued.

67

"Maybe it would help if we go over there," Frosty said.

"There's got to be an answer—a simple answer—if we can just figure it out."

They heard the captain get to his feet in the pilot house above them. Chong folded the map hurriedly and stuffed it into his pocket.

"I've got to get supper started, or I'll be in a real jam."

"We'll help you."

Chong cut up the vegetables and meat and dumped them in the large wok that served as a kettle. While he was doing that, Frosty made the tea, and Todd put the plates and chop sticks on the table.

"I sure wish we could go over to that temple tonight," young Roberts said.

"There's not a chance of that," Khoo Chong replied. "It'll be dark before we finish eating and the dishes are done and the galley's cleaned up. Besides, I wouldn't want to take a chance on going over there tonight." His voice lowered, and for an instant fear gleamed in his dark eyes. "The men who are watching our house in Singapore may have friends up here. It is better that we are careful so we don't get into trouble."

Todd shuddered. "You can say that again."

At the table that night, Yeo Seng Chi sat across from Frosty. He frowned his disapproval when Khoo Chong bowed his head to pray silently before eating. He said nothing all through the meal, and as soon as he finished eating, he got up and stalked out on deck. It seemed as though he wanted to have nothing to do with any of them.

The next morning the boys were going to leave for the

68

Buddhist temple as soon as breakfast was over, but Captain Tham had some work for Chong to do.

"That worthless Yeo Seng Chi took off during the night," he said. "Somebody on the crew's got to do his work." He squinted at Chong. "And I'm not going to. So you can guess who's going to take care of it."

Chong nodded. "I'll start as soon as I finish the dishes."

"We'll help you," Frosty volunteered.

The captain grunted. "I sort of figured on that, too."

7

Chong Attacked!

THE BOYS THOUGHT they would be finished with the deck scrubbing so they could leave the *Bird of Paradise* by midmorning at the latest, but Captain Tham kept finding things for them to do. He decided that all the glass on his boat had to be washed and the brass polished when they finished scrubbing the deck. Then the lines had to be re-rolled and stored below. It seemed to Frosty that he was deliberately trying to find things for them to do to keep them aboard. At last, however, they had all the work done.

"It's all right for you to go around town for awhile," the captain said grudgingly, "but see you're back here so we can have supper on time."

They started ashore.

"And mind you, see that you don't get into trouble," Captain Tham called after them. "I told Dr. Leng and the American I'd take care of you."

They were on the dock when Chong thought about their cameras. "Why don't you take them along?" he asked.

Frosty shook his head. "Not this afternoon." He hadn't thought they wanted to be bothered with cameras this time.

"You'd better have them." A strange tone of urgency crept into Chong's voice.

Todd went back on board. "I'll get them."

"What's all this about cameras?" Frosty asked, guardedly.

"You guys have got to look like tourists when you go to the temple," Chong whispered. "As long as you're snapping pictures of everything you see, nobody will think anything about your being there."

"What about you?"

"I'm Chinese. They'll think I came to worship."

When Todd returned, he and Frosty hung their cameras about their necks and set off with Khoo Chong. Three or four blocks from the temple, he left them.

"I'll meet you there. It would be best for us not to show up together."

"Have you got the map?" Todd asked.

"It's in a safe place," the youthful Chinese said cryptically.

"What're we going to do now?" Frosty asked.

"Try to figure out exactly where the jade carving is, for one thing. Then we'll come back here tonight when there's nobody around and get it." Then Chong melted into the crowd and was gone. For an instant the American boys stared up the street, trying to pick him out in the surging mass of people.

"I—I don't know whether I like this or not," Frosty Roberts said uneasily.

"We can't back out now," his cousin countered. "We promised."

Young Roberts glared at Todd. "Who's backing out? I just said I don't like it."

Frosty and Todd were delayed when they stopped to watch a fortune teller plying his trade. He was sitting across from a wizened old lady, trying to tell her how long she would live and what would happen to her by reading the lines in her hand. A few doors farther they saw a craftsman skillfully finishing the last details of an intricate dragon carving for the gates of a temple. And at the end of the block they saw a boy not much older than they were, spreading joss sticks on the ground to dry.

They were so interested in what was going on around them that they forgot Khoo Chong momentarily. They didn't remember him until they rounded the next corner and saw the temple in the middle of the block.

"Hey," Todd exclaimed, "We'd better get moving. Chong's probably waiting for us."

It was midafternoon, and the crowd at the temple half filled the courtyard. There were lines at the stalls selling food and oil for sacrifices and joss sticks and paper money. The money-burning furnace was pouring black smoke into the air. While they watched, two or three women and a man approached the furnace, paper burning in their hands, and threw it in to feed the hungry flames.

"What do they do that for?" Todd asked.

"The paper they're burning is supposed to represent money. And when they burn it, they believe they're sending it to their dead ancestors in the next world so they'll have money to spend."

"I thought that was what Khoo Chong said, but when I

actually see how it's done, I can't believe it," Todd went on. "I can sure see why his father became a Christian. It—"

His voice choked off suddenly.

"Frosty!" he whispered. "Look over there, will you?"

The Roberts boy stared at the temple doorway in the direction his counsin was pointing. "I can't see anything."

"I just saw Chong talking to some old guy. It looked as though he was trying to get away, but the character had hold of his wrist."

They moved forward, passing between the two carved granite lions. The boys were so excited about Chong they didn't think about the lions or the valuable artifact supposedly hiding there.

"I still don't see him."

"I don't see him now, but I did a second ago—I'd swear it!"

At that moment they heard a muffled cry.

"That's him!" Frosty exclaimed, speeding forward.

At the temple doorway, Todd caught a glimpse of Khoo Chong deep in the shadows. A powerful, angular individual had grabbed him around the waist and was jerking him toward a side room. The Chinese boy was struggling furiously to free himself.

"Let go of him!" Frosty shouted, rushing forward.

Without thinking, Todd threw his camera up and tripped the shutter. The flash briefly lighted the dark corridor and extended some distance into the little room. Young Roberts grabbed for the man's wrist in an effort to help free his friend, but the picture Todd had taken seemed to have more effect on him. With a snort of rage, he flung his captive away from him and made a leap to grab the camera. But Todd was too quick for him. He threw himself to one side to avoid the man's wild efforts and tightened his grip on his camera.

The man's hand found it and jerked at it frantically but the strap held. He whirled and went barreling through the crowd. It all happened so rapidly that the man's face was a blur to Todd. He hadn't been able to distinguish his assailant's features.

Frosty, who had been almost knocked down when their young Chinese friend was hurtled into him, got to his feet.

"What happened?" he asked. "Are you all right?"

By that time a crowd had started to gather, pushing close around the youthful trio, talking excitedly in Chinese. Two of the men wanted to know if they were all right.

"Sure," Khoo Chong said quickly. "We're fine. He just surprised us, that's all."

"We have thieves here on Penang," another Chinese businessman said in excellent English, "but to try to steal a camera in the daytime! That is something I have never seen before." He turned to Todd. "I wish to apologize for my countryman. Such an act brings shame to all of us."

Todd didn't know what he said in reply. All he remembered was that he grasped his camera with both hands and made his way through the curious onlookers. Chong and Frosty followed him.

"What're we going to do now?" his cousin whispered.

"We'd better get out of here fast," Chong said softly. "We've already attracted a lot of attention."

With that he left the courtyard, heading for the busiest street he could find, one where they could lose themselves quickly.

"We haven't done anything to be ashamed of," Frosty replied, "and we sure haven't broken the law."

"True, but if they haul us down to the police station it'll direct a little more attention to us and provide one more chance for the thieves who are after the jade carving to know that we're involved."

"If those thieves are anywhere around," Frosty observed, "they already know about us."

"Yeh," Todd said. "I might have gotten a picture of one of them."

"Hey, I hadn't thought of that."

"You saw him, didn't you, Chong?" the young Roberts boy asked.

"It was too dark where the guy was standing. He called to me as I was going by. When I turned toward him, he motioned for me to come closer. Then he grabbed me and you guys showed up." Their Chinese friend stopped suddenly. "Know something? That guy knew me! I just remembered. He called me by name!"

Frosty and Todd gasped.

"Then those thieves do know you're here—and why!" Frosty said.

"I don't see how they could have," Khoo Chong answered slowly. "We were most careful to keep it a secret. They couldn't know about my being here unless they missed me at home and guessed where I was. They're probably still watching our place, you know."

"Maybe it's somebody you know."

"It could be. That might be the reason he stayed so far

back in the shadows. He didn't want to be in the light so I could recognize him."

"It wouldn't be so hard to find out whether you know him or not," Todd said, his grin wide. "All we have to do is get the film developed and take a look at it."

They found a small photo studio on a side street in the business district and asked the clerk if it would be possible for them to get the roll developed and printed so they could have it the following day.

"I think so. We will try."

When they were out on the street once more Todd turned to his companions. "What're we going to do now?"

"I'll have to go back to the *Bird of Paradise* and fix supper," Chong said, checking the time. "We'll probably have to wait until tomorrow to go back to the temple."

The fat boy stared incredulously at him. "You don't really mean that you're going back to the temple again after what just happened?"

"I have to."

"Are you out of your mind?"

"I promised my father!" He drew in a long breath. "He is counting on me!" His gaze found Frosty. "But you don't have to go with me."

"Maybe not, but we're going, anyhow." He repeated himself for emphasis. "We're not going to let you go back there alone, are we, Todd?"

His cousin wiped the sweat from his forehead. "I—guess not. But how are we going to manage it without getting in trouble again? After what happened there a little while ago, they may know enough about where the jade carving is to know we'll be back to the temple."

"I hadn't thought of that," Khoo Chong replied thoughtfully. "You may be right. But, we're going to have to go over that courtyard again in the daytime. As soon as we can figure out exactly where the figurine is hidden, we can go back at night and get it."

Todd shook his head doubtfully. "You sure make it sound easy."

When they got back to the *Bird of Paradise,* Captain Tham was even grumpier than usual. He had been trying to get a hand to replace Yeo Seng Chi but hadn't been able to find anyone. He stormed about the little boat finding fault with everything Chong did.

"Why don't you tell him off?" Frosty asked after a particularly violent tirade.

"What good would that do?"

"It makes me mad just to listen to him tear into you." Frosty's cheeks were livid. "You'd be showing him you don't have to take it."

"He's just mad because Yeo Seng Chi left, that's all," Chong said mildly. "Besides, if I'm going to show him that Christ has made me a new person, I've got to act like it."

He said no more, but Frosty could think of little else. Khoo Chong was different than anyone else he knew. He had noticed it the first time they met, but he hadn't been able to understand it. He wasn't sure he understood it yet. It wasn't only that Chong was able to control himself. He actually didn't seem to be upset by the captain's explosions.

78

"Have you ever seen a guy like him?" Frosty asked Todd when they were getting ready for bed that night.

"I sure haven't." Todd untied his sandals and kicked them off. "Do you suppose that religion of his is what makes him the way he is?"

"Search me. He talks a lot about Jesus Christ, but he doesn't say anything about religion."

"You know what I mean."

They turned out the lights and crawled into their bunks. After a time the Roberts boy raised himself on one elbow.

"Being around Khoo Chong sort of makes you want to have what he's got, doesn't it?"

The silence was long and painful.

"I don't know," Todd murmured. "I haven't thought much about it."

Frosty knew that wasn't true, but he didn't challenge his cousin right then. He was too uncomfortable himself to find fault with Todd or anyone else. He kept telling himself that he was a Christian, too. He didn't have to change. But deep inside he knew it wasn't true. At least he didn't have what their Chinese friend had, that was sure.

Frosty tossed uneasily on his bunk for an hour or more before drifting off into a restless sleep. And when he woke up a bit earlier than usual, he was still disturbed.

Todd, on the other hand, was as chipper as ever. He got out of bed, dressed, and washed for breakfast. "Well, what do you think we'll find when we go to the temple today?"

"I hope we'll be able to find where the piece of jade is hidden and wind up the whole mess. I don't mind telling you, I don't like it."

79

"Neither do I. Besides, there are a lot of things around Penang I'd like to see and take pictures of." At the dresser he turned. "Okay, what did you do with it?"

Frosty's face looked up questioningly. "What're you talking about?"

"You know what I'm talking about. Where'd you put my camera?"

"I didn't have your camera. Did you look in your drawers?"

"I didn't put it in a drawer." Nevertheless, he jerked open his drawers and looked to be sure. "I remember thinking I'd need it today, so I laid it right up here."

"If you put it there, it still ought to be there." The Roberts boy got to his feet thoughtfully and started towards the dresser.

"Take a squint at this, will you?" Todd demanded, going over to the door of their little stateroom.

The lock had been pried off and now clung to the door by a single screw.

"Why would anyone do a thing like that?" Frosty asked. And then he remembered the picture Todd had taken. "Somebody stole your camera to keep us from seeing the picture you took of the guy who grabbed Chong!"

"That couldn't be," his counsin answered. "The picture wasn't even here. We left it at the studio to be developed."

"We know that, but the thief didn't."

Todd leaned against the table for support. "Man! Those characters would do *anything* to get that carving!"

8

A Meaningless Clue?

KHOO CHONG was already in the galley preparing breakfast when the American boys came in and told him about the door to their cabin and Todd's missing camera. His face registered no emotion, but Frosty saw that his hand trembled slightly as he measured the tea.

"I was afraid something like that might happen," he said. "The carving is so valuable they'll do almost anything to get it."

"Nothing else was taken from our room," Frosty said, "so he had to be after the picture Todd took of him. That makes me believe you must know the guy."

"Could be."

They were still discussing the theft when Captain Tham stalked into the galley.

"Is either one of you guys missing a camera?" he asked.

Frosty and Todd eyed each other curiously. They hadn't expected that.

"I am."

The captain flung it on the table.

"You're not going to have one if you don't take better care of it. I found it on the deck outside the pilot house door this morning."

"You did?" Todd exclaimed, picking it up. The hinged back swung open. "We thought it had been stolen."

"Stolen? That's a laugh!" The captain snorted. "Who would steal a cheap camera like that? You must've taken a roll of film out of it and dropped it or set it down."

Todd knew better and was about to tell him so, but Frosty and Chong both stared hard at him, warning him to silence.

"If that dad of yours doesn't come in a day or two, Roberts," the boat's owner and skipper continued, "I'm going to have to dump you two ashore and go back to Singapore. I can't wait around here much longer."

"Dr. Leng told you how long they would be gone," Frosty said. "Dad's paying you for waiting."

That seemed to stop Captain Tham momentarily. He picked up his teacup and held it in his hand. "Maybe so, but I'm getting tired of laying around like this."

As soon as he would allow Khoo Chong to leave the *Bird of Paradise* after breakfast, the boys went ashore and started for the temple.

"Why didn't you guys let me set Captain Tham straight this morning when he jumped me about my camera?" Todd wanted to know as soon as they were on the street. "Now he thinks I'm a jerk for being so careless."

"We wouldn't want to deceive him by making him think you're something else, now would we?" his cousin bantered.

"Besides," Chong added, "Captain Tham would be as curious as anybody about the theft. He'd want to know why your

84

camera was taken from your cabin and nothing else was missing. And why the thief would drop it on the deck after he went to all the trouble of stealing it. He'd have a lot of questions he'd want answered." The Chinese boy breathed deeply. "And right now, we've got enough problems without having to worry about anyone else finding out what we're doing."

They were a block or so from the wharf where the *Bird of Paradise* was secured when Frosty asked about the film they took to the photo shop for processing.

"Do you think the guy's got it developed by this time?"

"Probably not," Chong replied. "I don't think we can get them until this afternoon. Why?"

"If you could see that picture, you would know the name of one of the guys who's after the carving. It might be a big help. Maybe it would be enough for us to go to the police."

The Chinese boy nodded in agreement. "That's right. I hadn't thought of that."

Although it was still fairly early in the morning, the temple courtyard was crowded when they got there.

"What's going on?" Frosty wanted to know. "The place wasn't crowded like this when we were here yesterday."

"This is a holy day. There'll be more people coming here all the time."

Frosty looked across the courtyard at the surging multitude. Already the rusty iron furnace was belching smoke and the sweet-acrid smell of joss sticks and incense drifted out of the building to sting his nostrils. "We're not going to be able to do much today, are we?"

Chong hesitated. That had been his first reaction. Now that he thought about it, however, he began to change his

85

mind. "It might be easier with a crowd around than it would with the place empty."

They pushed their way into the growing mob of people.

"Everybody on Penang must be coming here this morning," Todd muttered.

Frosty had to agree with him. There were people everywhere.

There was a festive air about the courtyard as men and women jostled for position at the stalls to buy joss sticks or food for sacrifices. It seemed more like the Fourth of July at home than a religious holy day. Chong was leading them toward the carved granite lions that stood watch over the temple. They were still some distance away, however, when a girl of about eight approached Frosty.

"You want to buy lottery ticket?" she asked.

He shook his head, keeping an eye on his companions so he wouldn't lose them in the crowd.

"You buy lottery ticket and burn joss sticks," she informed him. "The gods will bring you luck and you win."

"No, thank you. It doesn't sound like much of a deal to me."

"You try lottery ticket one time. You see!"

He turned to face her. As he did so he caught sight of a man watching him from the far corner of one of the wooden stalls. The man ducked back quickly as their eyes met. He didn't get out of sight soon enough, however, to keep Frosty from realizing he had seen him before. Sweat broke out on the boy's lean face, and his shoulders quivered.

"I—I'm sorry," he blurted to the girl. "I haven't got time to talk to you." With that he hurried away.

"Just one ticket?" she called after him. "You buy just one—please?"

He found Chong and his cousin examining the marble base of one of the lions.

"There you are," Todd exclaimed when he came up. "We thought we'd lost you."

"I've got to talk to you guys," he whispered, bending toward them. "We're being followed."

Chong jerked erect, his features going pale. "Are you sure?"

"As sure as I've ever been about anything in my whole life. He was right over there by that paper money stand half a minute ago."

Todd straightened. "I don't see anyone."

"Of course you don't. He ducked out of sight as soon as I realized I'd spotted him."

The Roberts boy thought Chong would be as anxious to get out of there as he was, but surprisingly, he was in no rush. "Stand in front of me," he whispered, "and act interested in what's going on."

"What're you going to do?" Frosty knew he shouldn't have voiced the question. It popped out, unbidden.

Khoo Chong frowned his disapproval and looked away, his actions demanding his companion to control his tongue and stop asking such things.

He turned deliberately and surveyed the stalls, hoping he gave the appearance of being interested only as a tourist. He did not see the stranger, however. It was as though he had disappeared, swept away by the throng.

After half a minute or so Chong knelt as though to buckle

his sandals. Frosty couldn't understand why it took him so long, but when he finally stood erect, he was ready to leave.

"There's no use in our staying here any longer," he said, somewhat louder than he usually spoke. "We can come back and get some pictures when there are not so many people around. Okay?"

"Sure," the Roberts boy answered. "Anything you say."

They left the courtyard and retraced their steps towards the *Bird of Paradise.*

"What were you doing back there?" Frosty asked when they were alone.

"Trying to get the carving. I figured with all the people around the temple today, nobody would pay any attention to what we were doing." He went on to say that he had finally figured out where the map said the carving was hidden. "You remember the notation, 'second row, fourth over?'"

The Roberts boy indicated that he did.

"I woke up in the night thinking about it, and I realized that referred to the marble bricks in the pedestal that holds one of the lions. And I was right. It was loose."

"So that's what you were doing when you bent over to buckle your sandals?"

"Right. But I didn't find it." Chong frowned. "The only thing that was behind it was a piece of paper. That's all."

Frosty was disappointed, but the fact that there was a piece of paper there indicated Chong was making progress.

"What does it say?" he asked.

Their Chinese friend didn't know. "We'll have to get back to the boat first."

They were half a block past the photo studio when Todd insisted on going back to see if the picture was finished.

"It won't take ten minutes," he said.

"I've got to get back," Chong answered. "The captain will really be on my back if I don't have dinner ready for him at noon. You guys go ahead."

Frosty remembered the stranger who had been following them. "We could wait and go after we eat, if you think we should."

"Go ahead. You know how Captain Tham is. I might have to stay on board and work this afternoon."

The boys went over to the photo studio and asked about the prints.

"They are ready," the clerk said. "I will get them in one minute."

He returned in a short time and handed Todd the envelope. It was all the young Americans could do to keep from looking at them right in the studio. In fact, Todd started to open the envelope and would have examined the prints, but Frosty insisted on leaving.

"We've got to get back," he said. "We can look at those later."

"It'll only take a jiffy."

"Come on." He took his cousin by the arm and propelled him out the door. "We've got to get moving."

As soon as they got back to the *Bird of Paradise,* Todd hurried to their cabin and removed the prints from the envelope.

"These aren't half bad," he observed.

"Let me see them." Frosty jerked the pictures from his

cousin's hand. "These pictures aren't the ones we wanted. They were taken on board."

"I know that. I was just getting to the one at the temple."

The boys both groaned aloud. "Look at it!" Frosty cried. "It doesn't show a thing."

"It's a pretty good picture," Todd said. "The exposure's right."

"Yeh, it's a good picture all right—of the back of Chong's head and the man's shirt. It's not going to help us figure out who grabbed him, that's for sure."

Khoo Chong came in and looked at it as soon as he could. He was as disappointed as Frosty and Todd were. "That just about gives us zero for the day," he said.

"What do you mean?" the Roberts boy asked.

"The paper we found behind that marble brick isn't going to be much help, either." He took it from his pocket and handed it to Frosty. "If it does mean anything, I sure can't figure it out."

The young American unfolded the paper hurriedly.

"What is this?" he asked, staring at it. "Some kind of a joke?"

"That's what I wondered when I saw it. It sure doesn't say very much."

There was a crude drawing on the paper of a man lying down. Next to it there was a dragon's head, showing the first section of the body. There was a circle above the dragon. That was all.

"There are no characters or anything," Frosty observed.

"There doesn't have to be," Chong said miserably. "Some-

90

body else got there before we did and stole the carving. They left this piece of paper to taunt us."

Frosty was ready to agree with him, but Todd was not so sure.

"Take a good look," he said. "Isn't this the same kind of paper your grandfather used for the map?"

Khoo Chong studied it carefully. "You're right, Todd, it is."

Frosty said he couldn't see that had anything to do with the drawing being genuine. "A lot of things are written on the same kind of paper."

"That map is old," Chong said, "and so is this paper. I think Todd's got something. The drawing is genuine."

The Roberts boy picked it up and studied it once more. "But what does it mean?" he asked.

Chong shook his head. "I don't have a clue."

9

The Black Ball

A CABLEGRAM came from Djakarta late that afternoon informing Captain Tham that Dr. Leng and Frosty's dad would be in Penang the following evening. The owner of the *Bird of Paradise* was visibly shaken by the news.

"I'll have to be ready to leave here when they arrive, or I'll lose money," he said, starting towards the door. "And I still don't have anyone to take Yeo Seng Chi's place. I'm going to find a man, and I won't be back until I do."

He was on shore, and the boys thought he was gone for the rest of the afternoon and evening, when he came storming back to the galley door.

"And you, Chong!" he exploded, "I want you to stay on board until I get back. And that goes for you two as well. Understand?"

The boys stared questioningly at each other when he was gone.

"Why do you suppose he said that?" Todd asked.

Frosty had been wondering the same thing, but he didn't

have any answers. Captain Tham had ordered Chong around as though he owned him, but until now he acted as though he hadn't cared where he and Todd went or what they did. Suddenly he ordered them to stay aboard, too. It didn't make sense.

"I don't get it," Todd observed aloud. "I don't get it at all."

"I guess it doesn't make a lot of difference," Khoo Chong replied. "We can't decipher that picture puzzle—if it does have anything to do with where the carving is hidden—so we don't have any place to go tonight."

"Let's take another look at it."

The boys went down to their cabin and closed the door before getting the crude drawing out once more.

It was as meaningless to them this time as when they looked at it before. "If there was just some writing to give us a hint of what it means," Todd murmured, "we might be able to figure out the rest. But there's nothing. Absolutely nothing."

"I've thought and thought and thought about it until my head hurts," Chong said, "but I can't think of a thing in that picture that relates to any place in Penang."

"Let's take a look at the man who's lying down," Frosty suggested after a time. "What does that make you think of?"

"A hotel?" Todd asked.

"There are hotels all over the city," Khoo Chong said. "How would we figure out which one it is?"

"Is there a hotel here that keeps dragons?" Frosty asked, grinning.

"Very funny."

"I like to be helpful when I can."

"Well, you wouldn't get a gold medal for being helpful with that remark, let me clue you."

They were still looking at the drawing and talking about it when there were heavy footsteps on the deck above.

"Who do you suppose that is?" Todd asked.

"There's only one person it could be," the Chinese boy said. "That's Captain Tham."

Frosty listened intently. Khoo Chong had to be right. The captain was the only one who would tromp around so noisily. Still, he didn't think he would be back so soon. "He must've found a sailor to take Yeo Seng Chi's place."

"Or," Todd added, "he changed his mind about looking until he found someone."

Chong folded the drawing and put it back in his pocket. "I'd better go to the galley and start supper."

"We'll help you."

As they left the cabin, a shadowy figure moved up the passageway. Todd stopped suddenly, grabbing Frosty by the arm. "Did you see who that was?"

"Yeo Seng Chi!"

"What do you suppose he's doing here?" Fear chilled Todd's voice.

Frosty couldn't answer him. The same question was churning in his own mind. But Khoo Chong found nothing unusual about it. "Captain Tham probably hunted him down and talked him into coming back to the boat," he said.

"I hope that's all there is to it." He didn't voice his own thoughts, but he didn't trust Yeo Seng Chi.

95

The old Chinese sailor came to the galley to eat with them, but he did not speak, even when Captain Tham told how he had searched the streets of Penang until he found him.

"Tried to tell me he was sick," the captain bellowed, "but as soon as I offered him more money, he got well in a hurry."

Yeo Seng Chi glared silently at the owner of the powerful voice, pushed back from the table, and abruptly left the galley.

Captain Tham laughed.

After that nobody said much. As soon as he finished eating, the captain went to his cabin, leaving the boys alone.

"What do you think about Yeo Seng Chi?" Frosty asked. "Is he sick?"

"I don't know, but there's something wrong."

When the boys finished the dishes and went back to their cabin Frosty asked to see the drawing again. Khoo Chong spread it on the little desk and for a moment or two looked at it with Todd and him.

"I don't know what good it does to keep studying it. I don't know any more about it now than I did before." Chong went over to the porthole, staring out at the darkening harbor. "It has to mean something! But what?"

Frosty picked it up once more. "You know," he said, "this doesn't look like a man lying down. If it is, he's wearing a nightgown."

Chong turned slowly. "What did you say?"

Young Roberts repeated his statement.

"Let me take another look at that." The Chinese boy went back to the desk and bent over the drawings. "That's it!" he exclaimed. "It's got to be!"

96

"Whatever are you talking about?"

"This is the Wat Chayamangkalaram Temple, the Temple of the Reclining Buddha! And this dragon is one of those in front of it. You remember we told you my grandfather carved them?"

Frosty nodded, his eyes widening. "And you think maybe he fixed a place for the jade figurine in one of the wooden carvings?"

"Not exactly. But he was working around the place awhile after the carvings were finished. He supervised the work of putting them in place and seeing that they were properly painted. That would have given him plenty of opportunity if he hadn't prepared the hiding place for the figurine while he was working on the dragons in his shop."

"You're right about that." Frosty went back to the drawing once more. "But what does this circle mean?"

The Chinese boy frowned. "I haven't figured that out yet."

They talked it over excitedly and decided to go to the temple and look around.

"We may see something there that will give us a clue," Todd said.

"That's a good idea," Chong said. "And the sooner we can get over there, the better it'll be."

"If Captain Tham doesn't blow his stack about our going ashore. He told us to be sure and stay on board tonight."

"That was when he was upset because he couldn't get a sailor to help him. He may feel different about it now."

Chong went to the captain's cabin and told him they were going into town for awhile. Strangely, he made no comment.

He was sprawled on his bunk, his eyes half closed, and only grunted to his cabin boy.

"We'll be back in a couple of hours," Khoo Chong informed him.

Captain Tham swung his feet over the side of his bunk and sat up. "What do you expect me to do?" he snarled. "Wait up for you?"

The Temple of the Reclining Buddha was some distance from the dock. At first the boys were going to walk, but when they realized how far it was, they decided on crowding into a trishaw (a Malaysian pedicab).

The driver complained a little at having, to take three of them, but Chong talked him into it. There was a brief haggling over the price, and they got in.

"You have never been to see the reclining Buddha," the driver said in passable English. "No?"

"We're from America," Todd answered, indicating Frosty and himself.

He took them across the business district, along the row of hotels that skirted the bay and headed up to the temple. The boys chafed impatiently, so excited were they about reaching the temple and seeing if they could find the jade carving. They didn't mention it, however. They didn't say anything at all. When they pulled up in front of the gleaming temple, ablaze with lights, the driver turned to Chong. "You want me to wait?" he asked in Chinese. "I will take you back cheap."

"I don't——" He was about to send him away but changed his mind. If they did find the carving, they would want to get back to the boat as quickly as they could. "That would be fine. We'll be out in a little while," Chong answered.

The boys remained motionless at the curb for a time, studying the brilliantly painted building with its statues out front and the long dragons on either side of the walk.

Frosty's hand was trembling as he pushed his fingers through his hair and sweat pearled his forehead.

"Do you think we'll find it?" he whispered.

Khoo Chong moved forward hesitantly. "If we could only figure out what that circle means," he muttered aloud.

"Maybe it's one of those circles of carving in the peaks of the roof," Todd suggested.

But the other two didn't think so.

"I don't believe my grandfather would have put it up so high. He would have placed it somewhere that's easy to get at."

"Maybe it's on the inside," Frosty said.

Chong couldn't accept that, either. "This temple is quite a tourist attraction. There are always people going through, and there are guards inside." He shook his head. "No, it's got to be out here."

"But where?"

"That's what I can't figure out. There's got to be a circle here that we haven't found yet."

"The only circles I can see are those balls in the dragons' mouths," Todd observed.

Khoo Chong jerked to a halt. "That's it!" he whispered hoarsely.

"Do you really think so?"

"It's got to be! Grandfather carved the dragons with the pearls in their mouths for this temple. Those black balls represent pearls. He could have carved a hole in one of them to hide the figurine in."

Frosty nodded. Somehow he was sure they had deciphered the drawing correctly.

Todd looked at the brightly lighted building and the people who were coming and going. "How're we going to get it without anyone seeing us?" he asked.

"We can't do it now," Chong replied. "That's for sure. We'll have to get back here in the middle of the night when the lights are off and there's nobody around."

Frosty had an idea, however. "Let me try."

"Okay." Chong whispered a warning. "But be careful. We don't want to ruin everything now."

The American studied the two dragons carefully, as though he were more interested in the way the carving was done than in anything else at the temple. He looked at the long, sinuous body and examined the scales and the spikes on the back. People glanced at him as they walked by, but no one seemed to pay any attention to him. They were used to seeing curious tourists in Penang.

Finally Frosty reached the dragon's head. He looked at the eyes and the teeth and then took hold of the black ball in the fascinatingly ugly serpent's mouth. A moment later he was doing the same thing with the other dragon. His fingers were exploring the black ball that represented the pearl.

"It's no use," a man's voice said behind him. "You can't pull it out."

He jerked around to face the owner of the voice, his own cheeks pale with fright.

"Don't be so frightened," the slender Malay said to him.

100

"I only want to tell you that you can't pull it out. It's all carved from one piece of wood."

"I— I—"

The stranger was still laughing as he went inside.

Hurriedly Frosty rejoined his companions.

"Did you find anything?" Chong asked softly.

He nodded. "There's some soft stuff on the back of the ball at the top, but I didn't have time to dig it out."

"Then that's where the golden jade is," Todd said. "It's got to be."

"And we can't do anything about it right now," Chong added. "We don't dare try again when there's anybody around."

They left the temple presently and went back to the *Bird of Paradise.* Captain Tham was in his cabin when they went aboard, and Yeo Seng Chi was in his. Both rooms were well lighted.

"Remember," Khoo Chong whispered. "Don't say anything to anyone about where we were or what we found tonight. Okay?"

They nodded.

"What about the map and the drawing?" Frosty asked. "What're you going to do with them?"

Rather than stand out in the passageway talking, the Chinese boy opened his cabin door, and they stepped inside.

"I thought I'd hide them someplace until after we actually get the jade figure in our hands," he said.

They were still discussing it when they heard the boat engines start, vibrating softly through the deck.

"Hey!" Frosty exclaimed, jerking his head up and staring at his companions. "What's going on?"

"Captain Tham didn't say anything about putting out to sea!" Todd exclaimed.

"Let's see what's going on!" Chong strode to the door and jerked it open.

Yeo Seng Chi was glaring at him from the narrow passageway.

"Get back in there!" he snarled in English. "And be quick about it!"

10

Kidnapped!

KHOO CHONG did as he was told. The instant the door was closed the boys heard a key inserted in the lock, followed by the clink of metal against metal as the bolt was slammed in place. Todd grasped the knob and tried it, but it was no use. The door was locked.

"What's going on?" he whispered fearfully.

By this time they could feel the motion of the *Bird of Paradise* as she backed out of her berth, reversed engines, and began to creep through the still, moonless night.

"Why are we putting out to sea?" Frosty asked of no one in particular.

Actually, he didn't expect an answer. His companions knew no more about the reasons than he did. All they knew was that they were suddenly captive in Chong's cabin and their boat was moving slowly out to sea.

Khoo Chong went over to the porthole and looked out. By this time they were beyond the breakwater and the powerful searchlights of the harbor police.

"I've been expecting something to happen," he said. "But

105

I sure didn't think Yeo Seng Chi and Captain Tham would be in on it."

"Maybe the captain isn't," Frosty replied. "Maybe he's as much a captive as we are."

Chong made no further comment, but it was obvious that he did not agree.

The boys quit talking. They sat on the bunks in the little cabin, staring at the deck and at each other. "Do you really think they're after the carving?" Todd asked softly after a time.

Chong nodded. "What else would they care about that we might have?"

"But they haven't even searched us."

"They will," he replied. "They will."

Almost as though he had overheard them, the Chinese sailor appeared at the cabin door. He unlocked it carefully and opened it a crack.

"You!" he snapped icily, pointing at Todd, who was sitting the nearest the door. "Come with me!"

He did not respond immediately.

"You heard me!"

Nervously Todd shuffled towards the door. Yeo Seng Chi's hand darted in, grabbed the boy's wrist in an iron grasp, and jerked him out the door.

"Hey!" the fat boy sputtered, struggling to keep his footing. "I'll go with you. Take it easy!"

When he was gone, Frosty faced his Chinese friend.

"What do you think they're going to do to Todd?" he asked.

Chong's features were emptied of color, "I don't know. I hope they're just going to search him."

106

Frosty tried not to think of anything else that might happen.

"You'd better get rid of that map and drawing."

Even as Frosty spoke, Chong was opening the porthole.

And not an instant too soon. Somebody was at the door again, pushing back the bolt. Chong shoved the papers out the round hole and jerked it shut as the door opened.

"You, there!" A familiar voice rasped. "What're you doing?"

"Closing the porthole," Chong answered, simply.

Captain Tham blustered into the cabin. "Are you sure that was all you were doing?"

The Chinese boy did not answer him.

The captain strode into the cabin far enough to allow his companion to enter.

"Okay. Search the two kids and the cabin," he said to Chi. "It's got to be in here somewhere."

Chi set to work methodically. He searched Frosty and Chong hurriedly, making sure they didn't have the golden jade carving on them. The barefoot thief had finished with the Chinese boy, but Captain Tham made him hand over his wallet for inspection and turn his pockets inside out.

"That other kid said you don't have the carving, but we know better. Now hand it over!"

Neither Frosty nor Khoo Chong spoke or moved.

"We know you picked up that carving tonight. We're not going to let you go until we find it, so you'd just as well give it to us now and save everybody a lot of trouble."

They still did not answer him.

By this time the captain's associate had finished his search

107

and had found nothing. He had torn the beds apart, ransacked the drawers, and even opened the boys' cameras to be sure the valuable little figurine wasn't hidden inside.

"It isn't here, Cap," said Chi.

The captain swore angrily. "It wasn't in the other cabin, and it wasn't on the kids. It's *got* to be in here!"

Chi straightened and shrugged expressively. "Look for yourself if you don't believe me!"

"It's on the boat somewhere! It's got to be!" He leaned toward the two boys belligerently. "If we don't find it, we'll be back. Just remember that. We'll be back!"

As the captain and the old man left the cabin, Todd returned, pale and shaken.

"What did they do to you, Todd?" Frosty asked when the men were gone.

"N-nothing, really. T-they just searched me and—and threatened to throw me overboard if I didn't tell them where you hid the carving."

"What did you tell them?" Chong put in.

"I told them you didn't have it, that's all."

The frightened trio saw no more of the captain and his associate through the long night. They put the sheets back on the bunks and lay down. It was impossible for them to sleep, however. The throbbing engines kept reminding them of what had happened and that every turn of the propellers was pushing them farther and farther away from the Malaysian island.

"I just thought of something," Frosty murmured along toward morning. "When Dr. Leng and Dad get to Penang and can't find us, they won't have a clue of where to look."

"We won't even know where we are, ourselves," Chong replied. "Not that it would do us any good. We wouldn't have a chance of getting away from them as long as we're at sea."

Sometime during the night, the *Bird of Paradise* came to a halt at a little dock at an isolated island, and Captain Tham and Yeo Seng Chi forced the boys out of the cabin.

"Where are you taking us?" Frosty demanded.

The captain laughed scornfully. "That's none of your business. Just remember to be good little boys and don't cause us any trouble. If you do that, everything will be all right."

They took the boys about a mile up the beach to a decrepit little hut on stilts. Dawn was just breaking over the placid water, outlining the limits of the little clearing behind the cabin and revealing the slender fishing prau that was pulled up on the beach beyond the reach of the high tide.

"Now, remember Chi," the captain said. "Keep them inside with the door locked, and if they give you any trouble, call me on the walkie-talkie. Okay?"

He nodded.

"I'll call you every four hours, so have your set on. Understand?"

"Okay. Okay," the old sailor snorted indignantly. "You've already told me what to do."

"I know. I just want you to be sure to do it. I'll be back tonight to see how things are going."

Tham put the boys in the old cabin and locked the door before he left, giving the key to Yeo Seng Chi.

"Remember. Keep your eyes on them!"

The old man said nothing in reply. And with that final

109

word of warning, Captain Tham was gone, leaving Chi alone with the boys. The boys watched Yeo Seng Chi as he stood for a time in the shade of the cabin. Then he turned and disappeared.

"Where'd he go?" Frosty asked.

"Do you think he took off too?" Todd asked hopefully. "Do you think we can get away now?"

Chong hushed him with a wave of his fingers. Then he lay down on his stomach and peered through the cracks in the floor. Frosty and Todd joined him.

"He's still there," the Chinese boy whispered.

The old sailor was sitting crosslegged beneath the building, leaning up against one of the poles that supported it. Every now and then he closed his eyes, but he was not sleeping.

"We couldn't get a dozen feet away without his seeing us."

Todd was weighing their chances of escape. "But there are three of us and only one of him. If we jump him, he wouldn't have a chance."

"Maybe not," Chong said, "but don't forget that he's got that radio."

"We could take it with us," Frosty put in.

"You heard the captain make arrangements to call Yeo Seng Chi every four hours, didn't you? If he calls and doesn't get him, you can bet he'll be over here just as fast as he can." He shuddered. "And I'd hate to think what would happen when he found us."

"We can't just stay here and wait," Frosty reminded him. "You know as well as I do that we'll be in a real jam when they find out we don't have the jade figurine."

110

Todd looked up, his gaze narrowing. "We could tell them where it is," he said softly.

Both Chong and Frosty disapproved of that.

"If they get what they're after, there's no telling what they might do to us," the Chinese boy observed. "At best they'd go off and leave us without any food and no way out of here."

Then what *are* we going to do?"

Khoo Chong got wearily to his feet. "I don't know, but whatever we do, it's *got* to work!"

Yeo Seng Chi brought them breakfast and stood at the door while they ate. He grimaced as Chong bowed his head and prayed aloud.

"Keep us safe from harm," the Chinese boy began, "and help me to show Christ to Captain Tham and Yeo Seng Chi and the others by the way I act. Touch Chi's heart and bring him to the place where he wants to trust You as his Saviour—."

"Stop that talk!" the old man growled angrily. "I don't want you or anyone else to pray for me! You hear? I forbid it!"

Chong looked up but did not answer him. After that the old man seemed even quieter than usual.

That afternoon Captain Tham came back to the cabin alone, looking defeated.

"Did you find it?" Chi asked him in Chinese.

"It can't be in the boat! We've torn it apart and can't find it!"

"Talk to *them*." He gestured towards the boys with a quick jerk of his hand. "The owner was the grandfather of Khoo Chong. He can tell you where it is!"

111

Chong, who was listening to the conversation from the hut where they were being kept prisoner, shuddered. He didn't know what he would do if they started to question him seriously. He couldn't lie to them, but he couldn't tell them where the jade figurine was, either. Silently he prayed that God would keep him from such a situation.

"Dr. Leng is a friend of the Khoo family," Captain Tham continued. "We'll wait until he and the American get to Penang. Then we'll get word to them. They'll have to turn the carving over to us, or they'll never see the kids again!"

"I don't like it," Chi countered.

The captain swore at him. "Nobody asked you whether you liked it or not. All you've got to do is to follow orders."

Then the burly leader left, and Yeo Seng Chi was alone on the ground below the hut.

"What're we going to do now?" Frosty asked guardedly.

"If those guys are desperate enough to hold us for ransom," Chong said, "they'll do anything. We've got to get out of here, if we can."

"But we don't even know where we are," Todd protested. He was beginning to doubt the wisdom of leaving. "Where will we go, and how will we get there?"

"The first thing we've got to do is to get away from Chi. Then we can think about signaling a boat to help us get back to Penang."

The boys discussed their escape at length before Frosty came up with a plan that sounded feasible.

"The simplest plan is the best," he said.

Chong and Todd nodded in agreement.

112

"But what is that simple little plan?" his cousin asked.

"The door is held shut by a hasp and a padlock, right?"

"Right."

"And the termites have been working on the door and the casing."

"I hadn't noticed," Todd admitted.

"Take a look and you'll see that they have," Frosty said. "If we all throw our weight against it at the same time, we should be able to drive the screws out of the door or the casing. And we'll be free."

"You don't expect Chi to be standing around while all that's going on, do you?"

"If it works the way I think it will, we'll surprise him."

Khoo Chong considered the plan carefully. "It sounds good to me."

"It sounds all right to me, too," Todd acknowledged reluctantly. "When are we going to try?"

Frosty had been thinking about that. He was sure Chi would radio the boat as soon as they broke out of the hut and ran into the jungle. He was also sure that the men back at the *Bird of Paradise* would come as quickly as they could. Right now Frosty knew that he and his companions were the key to success as far as the thieves were concerned. Tham would have to take time to organize a search.

"The quicker we can get out of here," he said aloud, "the better it'll be."

Frosty took a look to be sure that Chi wasn't too close. "Okay," he whispered tensely. "Let's go."

The boys lined up opposite the door at the far side of the

113

little hut. Chong prayed hurriedly, asking God to help them get safely back to Penang. Then they burst forward at top speed.

An instant later they hit the door. The screws jerked half free of the wooden frame, and the entire hut trembled.

"Hey!" Chi cried as he heard the impact. "What's going on up there?"

"It didn't work!" Todd cried in desperation.

"Hit it again!"

This time the screws flew out of the hasp and the door flung open. Frosty wondered how Yeo Seng Chi had been able to run up the steps so quickly, because he was there! He had just reached the landing in front of the door when it swung open and the boys charged out. The door knocked Chi off balance, and the boys hit him full force an instant later, toppling him backwards off the steps.

A wild scream ripped along the beach and into the jungle. Chong stopped at the base of the steps.

"Come on!" Todd shouted to him.

Still the Chinese boy did not move.

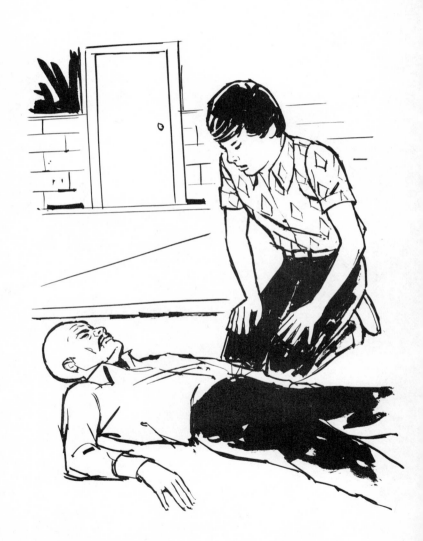

11

At the Temple Again

FROSTY was the first one down the steps. He dashed across the clearing and was about to go into the jungle when he stopped and looked back. Chong had remained at Yeo Seng Chi's side and was bending over him.

"Come on!" the Roberts boy called out impatiently. "We have to get out of here."

Their Chinese companion did not reply. Instead he knelt beside the elderly man who was sprawled motionless on the ground. "Are you all right?" he asked.

For answer Chi groaned.

"We've got to keep going!" Todd cried frantically. "We can't fool around here! If the captain and his men find us, we'll be in a lot more trouble than we are now."

"Help me get him up the steps and into the hut before you go," Khoo Chong said.

"What do you mean?" Both boys were staring intently at him. "You're going with us, aren't you?"

117

Chong shook his head. "I've got to stay here and try to take care of him."

"The captain will be along in less than an hour. Let him look after Chi. He's not our worry."

"You know Captain Tham as well as I do. He'll never do anything for Yeo Seng Chi. He'd go off and leave him here to get well on his own or die."

Frosty couldn't understand Chong. The old man had plotted with the captain to steal the most valuable thing his entire family owned. He had even helped kidnap them and was guarding them for Captain Tham. He sure didn't owe Chi anything. And besides, staying would mean that the captain would still hold Chong captive.

But Frosty couldn't go and leave Chong there alone. He turned back, reluctantly. "Come on, Todd. Let's help get Chi up the steps."

"Then we'll go on, won't we?"

Young Roberts shook his head.

"You don't have to stay," Chong reminded him.

"Neither do you." He bent to help pick up Yeo Seng Chi. "I don't like the idea any more than Todd does, but we're all staying together. If you don't go, neither do we."

The old man opened his eyes. "No," he whispered weakly. "Don't stay with me. Go, while there's time."

"We can't leave you here," Chong informed him.

The old man summoned all his strength to continue speaking. "There's a hut just up the beach half a mile," he whispered. "There's a boat there with a motor and gasoline. You can see Penang from the beach, and you should reach it in less than an hour."

118

Todd's eyes lighted. "What're we waiting for?" he demanded. "Let's get him up in the cabin and beat it."

"We could take you along," Frosty suggested.

"An old man like me?" Yeo Seng Chi spoke incredulously.

"Why not?" Chong echoed. "We'll go get the boat and come over here for you."

Chi shook his head. "An old man like me," he repeated. "And after all I did to hurt you."

The Chinese boy was not even listening to him. "We'd better carry him up the beach a ways," he said, "so we can hide him in case Captain Tham gets back before we do."

Chi had said the hut was half a mile up the beach. Actually, however, it was less than that. They burst through the tangled bush, and there it was, a house similar to the one they had just left. And out in front stood a long, slender prau, securely tied to a stake.

Frosty ran forward, splashing through the shallows to get to the boat. Todd and Chong were not far behind him.

"It's got a motor just like Chi said," he exclaimed. "And the gas tank is full."

"Now, all we've got to do is get it started," Chong said, "and get back to the place where we left him."

Chong, who had spent most of his life in Singapore, knew nothing at all about motors, but Frosty and Todd thought they knew enough about them to start the ancient one-cylinder engine.

"Think you can get it going?" the Chinese boy asked, uneasily.

"We'll soon know." Frosty adjusted the throttle, opened

the choke, and turned the engine over with the crank. On the second try it started, putting smoothly .

In a matter of a few minues they were back to the place where they had left Chi and had him loaded in the narrow wooden boat. The old man's face was drawn, and once or twice he groaned audibly as they moved him. But when he was in the prau and they were headed out to sea, he seemed to relax. For a long while he lay there with his eyes closed, breathing heavily.

"Think we'll make it?" Todd asked.

Chong nodded. "Captain Tham won't know where we've gone, and even if he guesses, it will take him so long to get back to his boat that we'll be out of reach."

After a time Yeo Seng Chi began to talk. "Why did you think of me, Khoo Chong?" he asked again curiously. "I joined Captain Tham in his plan to steal from you. I helped them take you captive and bring you to this island. I was guarding you in the hut. Why did you come back and help me, even risking getting captured again by the captain?"

The Chinese boy did not reply.

"Is it because of your God?" he persisted.

"It is because of Jesus Christ and the new life He has given me," Chong said truthfully. "I can't take credit for it."

But Chi was not satisfied. "You are different from the others," he said. "Watching you makes an old man want what you have." He paused. "You will tell me about this Jesus?"

While Frosty steered the long, cumbersome prau through the placid water, Khoo Chong explained the way of salvation to the old man. The two young Americans listened intently

120

as he told Chi that only by putting his trust in Jesus Christ could he be saved from the results of his sin.

" 'The wages of sin is death,' " he quoted, " 'but the gift of God is eternal life through Jesus Christ our Lord.' "*

Yeo Seng Chi turned it over in his mind. "Are you sure that's for an old man who has lived a life of wickedness?" he asked.

"It's for anybody who will accept it," Chong said. "It's for you and for Todd and Frosty, if they want to let Jesus Christ have full control of their lives."

Chi's voice was taut with emotion. "Yes," he almost whispered. "I want what you have."

Frosty's hands sweat. He, too, had seen the difference in Chong's life. He had never thought he was so bad. He didn't skip school or cheat or lie to his folks. In fact, if anyone had asked him, he would have told them, quite truthfully, that he considered himself to be good. But that was before he had seen the sort of life his Chinese friend lived and before he had listened to him explain what it meant to be a Christian.

When Chong finished praying with Yeo Seng Chi, he turned quietly to Frosty. "How about you?" he asked.

The Roberts boy had realized by then that he too wanted to allow Christ to give him a new life. As the question was put to him, he knew he could wait no longer. "I've been wanting to become a Christian ever since we met you and I started watching how you live and listening to you explain why."

"So've I," Todd broke in unexpectedly.

Before they pulled into the harbor at the island of Penang,

*Romans 6:23.

121

all three of Khoo Chong's companions had become believers.

Yeo Seng Chi's smile was broad as he thought about what had happened to him. "When Captain Tham found me in Penang and told me he had learned of the valuable jade carving your grandfather had and how we could be rich if we were able to steal it, I came back to help him," he said. "I thought I would be happy if I got the money." He breathed deeply. "Now, I have no money; but I am happy, no matter what happens."

"Then Captain Tham didn't have the idea of stealing the jade before we got to Penang," Chong said.

The elderly Chinese man shook his head. "No, he didn't know anything about it until he saw someone following you. Then he overheard a conversation and decided to steal the statuette himself. He cooked up some false charges of breaking and entering and had the men taken into custody who had been following you. He figured to let you bring the carving on board and then take it from you."

"When we came back last night after visiting the temple, he thought we had found it," Chong said. "Is that it?"

The old man nodded. "That was the reason we set out for the little island. We planned to take you over there, take the figure away from you, and keep you captive until we had a chance to get away. You would have been able to get back on a passing boat. But you didn't have the carving, and you managed to free yourselves sooner than we thought." He chuckled mirthlessly. "I can just see Captain Tham. I'll bet he's so mad his face is purple."

The boys hadn't been ashore on Penang long when Dr.

Leng and Frosty's dad found them. "Where've you guys been? We've looked and looked for you since we got in this afternoon, but we couldn't find the *Bird of Paradise* or anyone who knew anything about her."

"Yes," the Chinese scholar said, "where is Captain Tham?"

"That's a long story," Frosty replied.

When they were eating dinner in one of the hotels that evening, the boys related everything that had happened.

"And you still haven't located the piece of golden jade. Is that right?" Dr. Leng asked.

"We haven't actually had it in our hands," Chong said, "but we know where it is."

"For sure?"

"For sure."

"Then I think we should go and get it, don't you?"

They finished eating and went out to the Temple of the Reclining Buddha by trishaw. The normal evening crowd was there, but Dr. Leng and Mr. Roberts decided not to wait until it thinned out. They stood on either side of the huge, carved dragon's head, shielding it from the curious, while Frosty and Khoo Chong went to work. After a moment Frosty expelled his breath sharply.

"Everything okay?" his dad asked.

"Everything's okay."

Chong glanced down at the statuette of an elderly Chinese sage. Frosty had dropped into his hand the figurine that was going to pay for the new church back in Singapore.

"I'll say everything's okay," he murmured. "In fact, everything's great!"

A long silence followed.

"Know something?" Todd said finally.

"What?" Dr. Leng asked.

"I wish I'd eaten another piece of pie."